"I don't have to tell any of you that this is not a game. There are things out there that see humanity as playthings and cattle, to be used and abused however it amuses them. We are what stands between those monsters and the people of Baltimore. We do this at the risk of our lives and our souls. We fall, and the best that could happen is we die. The worst?"

Bianca's voice went sad and cold. Her normally light skin grew paler. "I've seen part of it, the gates of Hell and monsters out of nightmare. It's like looking at the surface of the ocean. There are depths we can't imagine and would go mad if we tried. And that's what we risk, drowning in an ocean of evil with no chance of rescue."

PADWOLF PUBLISHING BOOKS BY JOHN L. FRENCH

Past Sins
Rites Of Passage: a DMA casefile of Agent Karver and Bianca Jones (with Patrick Thomas)
The Grey Monk: Souls on Fire
The Nightmare Strikes
Bad Cop No Donut (editor)
Mermaids 13 (editor)
Camelot 13 (editor) – forthcoming

OTHER BOOKS BY JOHN L. FRENCH

Bianca Jones: Blood Is the Life
Bullets & Brimstone: a Mystic Investigators™ book (with Patrick Thomas) featuring Bianca Jones
From The Shadows: a Mystic Investigators™ book (with Patrick Thomas) featuring the Nightmare
Here There Be Monsters: a Bianca Jones collection
Paradise Denied
The Assassins' Ball (with Patrick Thomas)
The Devil of Harbor City
To Hell in a Fast Car (editor)
With Great Power (editor with Greg Schauer)

MONSTERS AMONG US

A Bianca Jones Collection

John L. French

PADWOLF PUBLISHING

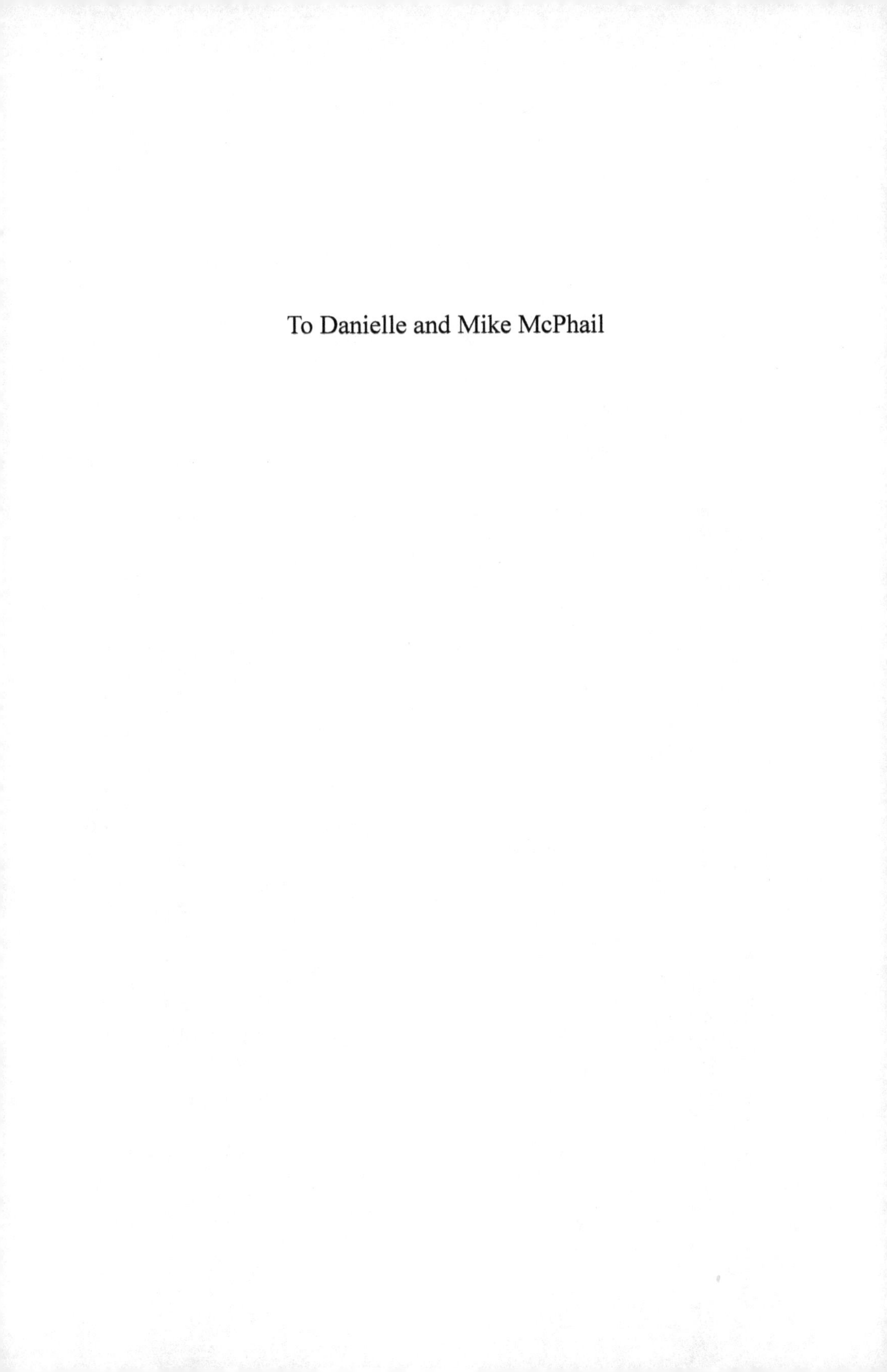

To Danielle and Mike McPhail

*Whoever fights monsters should see to it that i
n the process he does not become a monster.
And if you gaze long enough into an abyss,
the abyss will gaze back into you.
Friedrich Nietzsche, Beyond Good and Evil.*

THE CASE OF THE CURSED WEENIE

The story you are about to read is somewhat true, and could have only happened in Baltimore.

The city was covered in snow, thirty-one inches so far with more on the way. It was as if Hell had finally frozen and overflowed into Baltimore.

Maybe it has, thought Bianca Jones as she watched the third blizzard of the season from her bedroom window. What better way to paralyze a city?

Not so long ago Baltimore had suffered fires and riots. However horrible they had been, at least people had been able to act. Now everything was shut down and no one could move. If there were any predators out there the prey stood little chance.

The wind blew and in its voice Bianca heard the baying of the hounds of Hell. Though her room was warm a shiver ran through her.

It was not so long ago that she had fought and beaten demonic forces. She'd been to the Infernal City and had three times defeated its lord. That was supposed to have earned her city some protection against the Fallen One.

But for how long, she wondered. Baltimore might be protected now, but what about next year, or next month, or even next week. Maybe the talk about Baltimore being a charmed city was just that, talk, a ploy to get her to lower her defenses.

"Don't count on it," she said to the storm, using it to represent any supernatural force that might be planning to attack.

"Are you talking to me," came her husband's voice from their bed.

Bianca smiled. "It depends, Joe. What are you counting on?"

"You just got off duty. You've got twelve hours before you have to report back. You should rest or …"

"Or what?"

"You said things were slow. You can always sleep at work."

"Let me take a quick shower."

A few pleasant hours later, Bianca lay warm in her husband's arms. "So why were you talking to the snow?" he asked.

"Just something I'm planning for when this white shit melts. It's something I should have done a long time ago. Now let's have dinner before Beth arrives in the Humvee to pick me up."

***

Sliding up Walther Ave, dodging kids on sleds and trying not to hit idiots who didn't know how to drive in the snow, Gregory Tanner asked himself, "Just who did I piss off to get exiled to this God-forsaken city?" Then he asked, "And what's with all the lawn chairs in the street?"

Tanner knew the answer to the first question. Mitch Holder, his immediate boss, his one-time friend, had been responsible for the transfer. True, maybe Tanner should not have boffed Mitch's secretary. But how was he to know that Mitch was doing her too? It was an honest mistake and Tanner thought Mitch had overreacted about what was, after all, just a piece of ass, and a not very good one at that.

Mitch probably had orders from above, Tanner thought just as an orange traffic cone blew out in front of him. He braked, skidded, and almost hit an old lady who had run out into the street to retrieve it. She glared at him as she placed it back in her dugout parking spot.

"Just what is it with these cones and chairs," Tanner asked again. He would soon find out the hard way.

Pulling off Walther, Tanner found that snow on his street had melted just enough for his SUV to get up it.

"What kind of city is this?" he complained to his own personal gods. "Shitty public transportation, no decent snow removal and ..." Tanner looked around. The home he had had less than a week to find and buy did not have a driveway. "...there's no goddam place to park."

There was one empty space, empty but for three plastic lawn chairs. Good enough, Tanner decided and got out to move them.

"That isn't done around here." The warning came from Jamal Poole, a tall, thin, black man wearing several layers of clothes, thick gloves, and what looked like a very warm hat.

"What isn't?" Tanner was in no mood to be lectured by a near stranger.

"Mr. ... Tanner, is it? Here in Baltimore, you dig out a spot in the snow, you mark it with chairs and it's yours. Ain't nobody supposed to take it. Come on, I'll help you dig out a spot for your car."

Tanner didn't want to dig out a spot. He wasn't dressed for the weather and he hated hard work. "Blocking a parking space. That's illegal, isn't it?"

"Kinda, but in this weather custom beats law, even the mayor said so."

Tanner shook his head, said, "Screw it" and started to move the chairs.

Another warning came from Poole. "You do know that's Miss Solomon's spot, don't you?"

"And who the hell is Miss Solomon?"

"Hell may be right. She's someone you don't want to mess with."

"Screw Miss Solomon." Tanner got back in his car, parked it in the now open space. As he walked to his house, he added, "And screw you, and screw this crazy city."

Jamal Poole watched the doomed man go inside. Better call some of the neighbors, he thought. If we don't want this snow to last longer than it should, Miss Solomon better find an open space when she gets home.

* * *

The streets, while not entirely cleared, were at least passable enough for the men and women of the BPD to return to their regular shifts and duties. Bianca wasted no time in putting her idea into action.

She looked at the people gathered in her office. Homicide detective Bethany Steele, Lieutenant Tavon Greggs of the department's Quick Response Team, and forensic specialist Tammy Dolan. They each had their own duties but had become involved in Bianca's struggle against the weird and the strange.

When did I get a team, she wondered. It was supposed to be just me risking all to protect this city from the darkness, well, me and Morgan. Then it was Joe, then Beasley. Morgan died and I almost lost the other two. So what right do I have to ask these others to risk their lives and their souls fighting what might be an unwinnable war?

"Because without help you'll fail, then we're all damned."

Bianca had discussed her idea, and her doubts, with her husband the night before and that was what he told her.

"Even with a team I might fail. What then, Joe?"

"Working alone and without back-up? Like I said, we're damned. On a team, one person falls, the others carry on and get the job done. Or don't you like the idea that you may not be indispensable?"

To this Bianca had no answer, nor did she reply when Joe went on. "Get things up and running, find someone who could take over for you and is willing to do so. Then maybe we can have a normal life, a normal family life."

There was that word, "family." Bianca knew that Joe wanted one; part of her did as well. But there was another part of her that was afraid for any child she might have, afraid of it being hostage to the evil she opposed and more afraid that it might follow in its mother's footsteps.

Bianca stayed quiet and, smart man that he was, Joe did not press her. There's still time, he told himself, and prayed that it was true.

What right do I have, Bianca asked again and realized that right or wrong played no part in this. Just as she had been dragged into this crusade, so had circumstances brought these people to her.

"In the past year or so, we've all been involved in some way or the other with some crazy stuff. Monsters from books and other dimensions, vampires, frankensteins, assorted freaks, and the Devil himself."

"Not to mention fairies," this from Bethany Steele.

"Or fire demons," added Greggs.

"Negral's a fire god, Tavon, not a demon, and he's on our side."

"So you say, Bianca, but he still works down below. He shows up, I'm loading the blessed ammo you got from the Vatican."

"Not a bad idea, and that's the whole point of this meeting. Up until now, we've been making things up as we went along, facing unworldly and ungodly threats with courage and knowledge but damned little planning. We've been lucky. Well, we can't stay lucky forever. If Negral had been the demon Tavon thinks he is, if I hadn't been with Beth when the fairies came through, if … you get the picture."

"So what do we do?" Tammy asked.

"If Negral was right, beating back Hell's attack has earned Baltimore an indefinite period of Grace. How long we stay Charmed City …" Bianca shrugged.

"We use whatever time we have to prepare. We picture the worse threats possible and plan how to counter them. We imagine the most horrible monsters and come up with ways of beating them. No more going blind into a situation and hoping for the best."

Bianca gave her orders. "Tammy, take what you know about forensic science and figure out how to apply it to things not quite human. If something strange comes in I want to know what it is.

"Beth, check Lotus Notes every day for weird or odd cases, however minor. You or I will investigate and hopefully stop some stuff before it grows too big to handle. And for those cases that are …

"Tavon, start stockpiling guns and ammo, the bigger the better. I want you and your men to be able to blow holes in damned near anything, especially the damned things. In the meantime, Joe and I will start work on identifying possible targets. Hopefully some of the books he's got in his bookshop will tell us how to protect them."

Now for the hard part, Bianca thought. "I don't have to tell any of you that this is not a game. There are things out there that see humanity as playthings and cattle, to be used and abused however it amuses them. We are what stands between those monsters and the people of Baltimore. We do this at the risk of our lives and our souls. We fall, and the best that could happen is we die. The worst?"

Bianca's voice went sad and cold. Her normally light skin grew paler. "I've seen part of it, the gates of Hell and monsters out of nightmare. It's like looking at the surface of the ocean. There are depths we can't imagine and would go mad if we tried. And that's what we risk, drowning in an ocean of evil with no chance of rescue. If anyone wants out, now or ever, just the say the word and we'll wish each other luck."

The room was silent until Greggs spoke for everyone. "How big do you want the holes?"

***

Time passed and the snow melted. On Gregory Tanner's block it melted faster than expected, except in front of his house. There it lasted long after all the other snow had gone, melting just enough during the day to freeze overnight and make his front walk a treacherous slip-and-slide. Finally however, the sun prevailed and his yard was freed from winter.

That was the day Tanner left his house only to find a middle-sized, slightly overweight woman dressed in very bright colors waiting for him on his sidewalk.

Her skin was dark. Her face bore the traces of Arabia, the Congo, and the American South. When she spoke it was in a voice that had in it equal parts of the Caribbean, New Orleans and the Outer Banks.

"I have been waiting, Mr. Tanner," she said, confronting him on the sidewalk.

Tanner snarled at this stranger. "Waiting for what, and who the hell are you?"

"I am called Delilah Solomon and I am waiting for your apology."

"Apology for what, I never … oh, the parking space. That was weeks ago and you got another one."

"No thanks to you. The others, they know what is good for them, they show the proper respect. You did not, you do not. You took from me what was mine and for that disrespect I ask you to apologize."

The smart thing for Tanner to do would have to been to utter a sincere-sounding "I'm sorry, I didn't realize the custom. It won't happen again" but that phrase, those words were not in his vocabulary. Apologies, admissions of mistakes, anything like that were signs of weakness, and Gregory Tanner did not see himself as a weak man. He would not, could not back down, not to a crazy lady in a quilt of a dress, especially not in front of the neighbors who he was sure were watching.

This Solomon woman was blocking his way, keeping him from his car. He thought to push her aside but there were the neighbors, no doubt peeking out from behind their curtains. She'd claim assault, they'd back her up, and he would be calling in sick from a jail cell. Instead, with a "Go to Hell, lady" he walked around her.

"Hell is not a pleasant place, Mr. Tanner, as you will one day learn."

"Yeah, yeah." Tanner waved her off and continued toward his car.

Delilah Solomon followed him. "You think you are a big man with big plans. After today you are not so big."

Standing in front of his car, she took something long and white from a voluminous pocket in the front of her dress.

"Gregory Tanner," she said solemnly, "you took from me so I take from you." Strong hands broke the bone in two. "I curse your weenie."

With that she was gone. Relieved that the show was finally over, Tanner drove to work, his only thoughts being "I have got to get out of this city" and "At the very least, I have to move." To Miss Solomon's curse he paid no heed at all. Curses and those who cast them were not part of Gregory Tanner's world.

***

It was his girlfriend of the moment who first noticed the change. "You seemed smaller," she said after a bout of amorous activity. "Is everything all right?"

Tanner's first thought was to lash out, make some reference to her getting bigger and looser. His second was to imply that if she had been better he would have been bigger. Not wishing to be thrown out of her apartment and on to Saratoga St, he simply shrugged and said, "Tired, I guess."

Two nights later. "You are smaller," she said, lifting her head from his lap, adding quickly, "Not that it matters to me."

Tanner looked down. She was right, there was a visible difference. He was at least an inch shorter, maybe two. Only then did the words of a crazy lady in a brightly colored dress come back to him. "I curse your weenie," she had said.

No way, the practical part of his brain argued. Not possible, the logical part agreed. But then a forgotten, more primitive part came to the fore and as it flooded his mind with ancient fear, he heard his girlfriend suggest,

"Maybe you should see a doctor."

As he wilted beyond any chance of revival, Tanner somehow knew that he was beyond the help of Western medicine and wondered what to do next.

***

What Tanner did was to call the police, but he did so from his office, thinking it best if neither his neighbors nor that witch Solomon saw him talking to the cops. The officer who responded listened patiently to his tale, his face darkening when Tanner told him about moving the lawn chairs. When Tanner finished, the cop shook his head.

"You're from out of town, right?" Officer Calvin Rico asked. When Tanner nodded Rico went on. "Let me tell you something. Baltimore is one of the most violent cities in the country. People here get shot over twenty cents, stabbed for a pen, and killed over the last hard crab. And yet everywhere in the city, lawn chairs in the snow are sacred. The nicest guy, the worst punk. The preacher and the dealer. Nobody moves the chairs. Those that do …" The cop shook his head. "If you'd have been given a beatdown in front of twenty witnesses none of them would have spoken up for you. And if brought to trial, a Baltimore jury would have acquitted your assailant."

Rico filled out a Victim's Information form and handed it to Tanner. "For what little good it will do you, I'm gonna write up an assault complaint. Here's the report number. You can take it to a court commissioner and swear out a warrant. If you think that's the smart thing to do. Taking a parking spot cost you a couple of inches. Lock this woman up and she might make it fall off."

Something in the officer's voice caused Tanner to ask, "Wait, you believe me? You believe that she cursed my … um," Tanner looked down at his lap.

Rico shrugged. "That she cursed your pecker? Why not? This is Baltimore. Stranger things than that have happened."

Laughing to himself, Rico went back on patrol. Guys at the district are gonna love this one, he thought. Of all the weird shit. Rico then remembered other weird things that had happened, or were said to have happened, in the city lately. Vampires and werewolves, movie stars who walked out of burning buildings and houses that disappeared. A guy from the Southwest said there had been one of those in his sector. He said that late at night you could hear the screaming of those who had been inside when it vanished.

Rico started thinking that maybe this was more than just a guy who needed double Viagra. He vaguely recalled an email about strange and unusual occurrences. He'd check with his sergeant when he got off patrol.

***

Standing naked in his bedroom, Gregory Tanner looked in the mirror and willed himself hard. It didn't work. Neither had magazines, dirty movies, or Internet porn – not anymore. They used to, but each time he would look down at his shortened staff and …

Maybe it will grow back, he thought. Maybe I should apologize to the damned witch. Instinctively Tanner knew that it was probably too late for that, that Solomon would know that he wasn't sincere, that she would laugh at him. Or she might agree to restore him then set a price too high for him to pay.

He looked at himself again. Was there too high a price? How many thousands per inch would she charge? Or would she demand of him some service, or even his soul?

Tanner was torn between trying to convince himself that God and thus souls did not exist and wondering if there was some religious ritual that could restore him. Since his problem involved sex he rejected the Catholics and was leaning towards the Mormons – with all those wives they must have some kind of prayer for problems like his – when the telephone rang.

"Gregory Tanner?" asked a woman's voice.

"Yes?"

"This is Detective Bethany Steele of the BPD Special Operations Unit. I'm calling about your assault report against Delilah Solomon. We'd like to talk to you about it."

The words of Officer Rico came back to him. "Lock this woman up and she might make it fall off."

"Well, the thing is, Detective Steele, I've decided not to press charges."

"That's your right, Mr. Tanner, but this is part of an ongoing investigation. We'd appreciate your cooperation. You can either come to our office at your convenience or …" there was a deliberate pause, "… we'll send a patrol car to your house every day until we find you at home. Your choice."

"Not much of one," Tanner almost complained but instead he made an appointment for the next day at nine a.m.

* * *

How many people know? Tanner wondered as he entered the Fayette St. entrance of the police headquarters. Was that a funny look from the security officer when he asked for the Special Operations Unit? Was that a smirk on the face of the detective who let him into the office? Did the secretary look at his crotch and feel pity for him as she said, "Sergeant Jones will see you now." Whoever this Sergeant Jones was he better be able to help.

"Good morning, Mr. Tanner. I'm Bianca Jones."

Whoever Tanner had expected "Sergeant Jones" to be, it was not the person who greeted him – a young woman not more than five foot tall, looking like some teenager playing police. Ignoring her outstretched hand, Tanner just stared.

Bianca knew what Tanner was thinking as he looked her over. It was the same thing just about everyone thought. Too small, too thin, no shape, no boobs – she's a kid, she can't be a cop. She shouldn't be a cop.

Until they got to know her. Then they either liked her, respected her, feared her, or hated her. Bianca didn't care which.

The triple blizzard, lawn chairs and parking, weird neighbors, the curse, and now some kid cop. It was all too much for Tanner.

"Is this some kind of joke?" he blurted out, suddenly believing that the entire city had gone mad and was out to get him.

"Is that what your girlfriend asked you last night?" is what Bianca felt like saying and what she would have said had Tanner been a fellow officer. Instead she forced herself to be reasonably polite and replied,

"I find nothing funny about my size, Mr. Tanner. Now please sit down so we can discuss your problem."

All Tanner had heard was "size" and "problem." Remaining standing he said, "Young lady, I want to talk to your supervisor."

"Mr. Tanner, my only supervisor is the Police Commissioner and he can't help you. No one can, except me. And right about now I'm not sure I want to. So either sit down or get out. I really don't give a damn."

As much as he didn't want to admit it, Tanner realized that Bianca Jones was perhaps his only hope of returning to normal. Forcing himself to be calm, he sat down.

"It's the pressure, Detective Jones." And having learned something in the past few days, added, "I'm sorry."

Despite knowing that Tanner's apology came only from his fear and his need, Bianca nevertheless accepted it as if it had been sincere.

"That's what you should have said to Ms. Solomon. Instead, despite a warning from Mr. Poole, you pissed off a witch and got yourself cursed."

"You know about Poole? But how?"

"We're the police. We investigated. That's what we do. But don't worry, we were very quiet and discrete."

"Can you help me?"

"To be honest, I don't know, but I'm going to try. At the least, with your help, we may put a stop to Ms. Solomon's unauthorized witchcraft. Now then, tell me what you said to her, what she said to you, and exactly how she cursed your weenie."

***

"Tell me again how going to this witch's house is part of your new policy," Joe Russo said when Bianca stopped at his bookstore to take him to lunch. "It sounds like your usual 'barge in and hope for the best' plan."

"That's always worked before," Bianca said. "The Eichenkranz sound good for lunch?"

"The Eichenkranz sounds great, and please tell me you're joking."

"Only partly. I'm going to her house, but Beth has done a full investigation. Tavon will be standing by with some new toys to blow her to Hell if need be and I've got Tammy on garbage detail."

Joe was retired from the Crime Lab; he knew what the garbage detail involved. "I bet she loves that idea. What are you hoping she finds?"

"Enough to give me an edge. And that's where you come in, you and your collection of scary books."

"I've told you before, it's a library of esoteric and occult literature."

"With which you have a physic link. That makes them scary books. Let's go eat."

Over lunch, Bianca told Joe of her plan. "She's probably too smart to leave any hair or nail clippings," Joe said when she had finished, "but DNA and fingerprints are a different matter. What did Steele find out?"

"Solomon moved in about a year ago. At first her 'requests' were the usual new neighbor ones – leave the parking space in front of her house open, no loud noises, kids and pets off her lawn."

"And then."

"Some kid ran through her back yard. He tripped on nothing at all and broke his leg. A car parked in front of her house. All its tires went flat. And then a stray dog dropped a load on her front lawn."

"What happened?"

"It exploded."

"What!"

"Yeah, it went boom and rained doggie bits down on the sidewalk and grass. The neighbors dialed 9-1-1 but none of the calls went through. After that the requests became more specific."

"Such as?"

"How nice it would be if someone would cut my grass or wash my car. My house could use a new coat of paint. Could someone pick up my groceries? At first the neighbors ignored her, or tried to, but Solomon went biblical on them – plagues of ants, mice and other pests; grass that wouldn't grow and snow that wouldn't melt. Storms that damaged certain houses but left hers alone. Soon the neighborhood got the message. Those that could moved. The ones who couldn't went along."

"So they live in fear."

"Not as long as Solomon gets what she wants. She's a terrorist, Joe. She blew up a dog and maimed a man. What happens the next time she's not happy? She might cripple a kid or destroy a home. She needs to be reined in."

"Not stopped, just reined in? Why not drop a house on her?"

"She's got power, Joe, power we could use."

"If the price isn't too high. Be careful, Bianca."

"I'll be okay. After all, I don't have a weenie to curse."

"Yes you do, mine. So please, be very careful."

***

The sun was just setting when Bianca went to Solomon's house. Evening was her favorite time, neither day nor night, when neither the light nor the darkness ruled. All was in flux and anything was possible, such as a mortal confronting a witch and walking away unscathed. While she had faith in her preparations, Bianca would take any edge she could get.

She had thought to send Greggs in first, imagining his Quick Response Team pulling up in large black trucks and emerging laden with heavy weapons, with a police helicopter hovering overhead, contributing to the drama.

Not a good idea, she decided. Such a show of force would either immediately put Solomon on the defensive or imply that the BPD feared and respected her power. Bianca didn't want to do either.

"You and your men wait around the corner," she told Greggs.

"How will we know to move in?" he asked. "Steele says this witch can mess with communications."

"If you don't hear from me in thirty minutes, move in and level the place. I'll be past caring."

"You should let me do that now, Bianca."

"I don't want her dead, Tavon. I want her on our side."

Bianca walked up to the Solomon house alone. Knocking on the front door, she waited to be admitted.

And waited, and waited, and waited.

Finally the door opened.

Delilah Solomon was as Tanner had described, a dark-skinned woman in bright clothes and of many cultures. When she spoke it was in a voice for which many an actress would have sold her soul.

"You are the police?" she asked, blocking the doorway with her body.

"I am," Bianca admitted.

"You are armed?"

"Of course, I'm a cop."

Solomon shrugged as if to say that Bianca's gun, and thus Bianca, was no threat to her.

"You do not come as a guest." It was less a question than a statement of terms. Neither would owe the other anything – not service, not protection, not even simple courtesy.

"I've come to talk. If those are your conditions I must accept them," allowed Bianca.

"Then enter freely and at your own risk."

There was nothing special about Solomon's living room, except that Bianca had not thought a witch would shop at Ikea.

"This is about that fool Tanner."

"Only partly, Miss Solomon. This is about your practicing witchcraft in my city."

Solomon's brows lifted, her eyes widen and an amused smile appeared on her face. "Your city? Who gave it to you, little woman?"

"I took it. Took it under my protection to guard it from otherworldly threats."

"And am I one of those threats, small one?"

Normally very sensitive to remarks about her height, or lack thereof, Bianca forced herself to ignore Solomon's insults. Instead she took a deep breath and calmly said, "There are those who think that. I would rather have you as an ally, working with me to keep this city safe. In exchange …"

Solomon squared herself up. So much for talk, Bianca thought. Get ready for the rough stuff. Had Solomon been an average street punk, Bianca would be waiting for her to pull her piece. A gun would be easy, compared to the weapons this woman had. Bianca prayed her defenses were strong enough.

The smile left Solomon's face. "I have no interest in keeping this city safe or working with anyone. I will do what I want; take what I want from anyone I want. And cursed be she who would refuse me."

Bianca answered the challenge. "And I will do what I must, against anyone who would use her power for evil purpose. And damned be those who would stop me, Mari Beverly Mercer."

Bianca threw Delilah Solomon's legal name at her, the name on her birth certificate, the one given to her at birth. It had come from a fingerprint Tammy had lifted from a soda can found in Solomon's trash. And if what was in Joe's books was correct, the use of Solomon's true name would give Bianca power over her.

The smile on the witch's face returned and grew wider and wider until her lips parted and out came a laugh, a loud, long laugh that filled the room.

"Oh, little woman, you think to use my name against me. Is that what the pretty one was doing with my trash, finding my true name? Let me tell you of my name, small one. When I was a babe, my mother took me to the River. There she blessed me with its muddy waters and whispered into my ear my one true name. It was a name that I was too young to understand, a name that only she and the Bright One would ever know. I will learn my own name only when I pass over; until then it is my great secret, and my great power. Power you must now learn to respect and fear."

The air around Solomon shimmered and the smell of ozone filled the room. Bianca knew whatever the witch was conjuring was no simple curse. With no time to draw her pistol, Bianca hoped that Joe had been right about the other thing.

The power hit her.

Bianca had once been in an automobile accident. The airbags had gone off, leaving her bloody and bruised. She had once been shot, the bullet smashing against her body armor, again bruising her and that time cracking a rib. Whatever curse or spell the witch had thrown at her was worse. It was double the force of the bullet, triple that of the airbag. It was standing naked against a hurricane or having a mighty wave crash over her.

With the witch's power came an image of what was to happen. Bianca would be thrown back by the force, many of her bones breaking as she hit the far wall. She would lie there in pain until the witch tired of gloating, then her lifeless body would be thrown into the street like so much garbage.

When she was hit with the airbag, Bianca was forced back. When she was struck by the bullet, Bianca was knocked down. Both of those incidents left Bianca bruised and bloodied. Still, after the accident, Bianca had gotten out of her car and arrested the other driver. After she was shot, Bianca had gotten up and took down her shooter. This time, though again bruised and bloody, though again driven backwards and to her knees, Bianca withstood the blast. Standing by the force of her own will she resisted the power of the witch until it was spent.

Then it was just two women standing in an eerily undamaged living room.

"I have more than your true name, Delilah Solomon," Bianca said quietly. "I have your true self."

Bianca thought of how Tammy had extracted the witch's DNA from cans, bottles, pencils and other objects the woman had discarded. She thought of how Joe had incorporated this genetic material into a protective amulet, which Bianca was now wearing. Appreciating the irony of how the witch's very essence was protecting her, she felt Solomon's power filling her.

How good it was and what good she could do with it. Let monsters come, she would destroy them. Let the Devil return, she would blast him back to Hell. Let those who would defy her, fear her.

And so are evil witches born, the rational part of her soul warned.

Rejecting the power and all it promised, she sent it back towards Solomon in one mighty burst.

The force threw the unprepared witch into the far wall, possibly breaking many of her bones. As Solomon lay there in pain, Bianca approached, her gun drawn.

"You cannot hurt me," she told the witch. "Not in my city. Here I can do what I must. I can finish this now, finish you now. No one would care. But I offer you one chance. Swear by your unknown name to serve the city and I will get you medical attention. Refuse and I'll not suffer you to live."

"The Bright One," Solomon whispered painfully.

"If he shows up I'll kick his ass. Now what is your decision?"

No reply. The witch's killing blow had done its work. Delilah Solomon had learned her true name.

* * *

Recuperating at home, Bianca was enjoying being waited on. "Who is this 'Bright One' Solomon mentioned," Bianca asked her husband as he brought her another cup of tea.

"No idea," Joe replied. "There's nothing specific in the books. Maybe it's just another name for our friend down below."

"A worry for another day, and something else to plan for. Has Tammy called in?"

"Twice. The autopsy results are in. Delilah Solomon is really most sincerely dead. Officially of a massive stroke. Unofficially, every bone in her body was broken and most of her internal organs ruptured. You were lucky, Bianca."

"Luck had nothing to do with it. It was my faith in you. But you said Tammy called twice?"

"Only because Tanner's called three times. What are you going to tell him?"

"I was hoping that Solomon's death would restore him. Guess it didn't. In that case, we fall back on the fairy tale ending."

"Which is?"

"To break the curse he must win the love of a good woman who will accept him as he is."

"Is that true?"

"Of course, Joe. Once blessed with True Love, Tanner will realize that the little things don't matter."

A PLAGUE ON THE LAND
A story of *The Nightmare and Bianca Jones*

Everyone needs a place to unwind, to relax after a long night at work, to meet with those who share similar interests and to discuss common problems. After hours, when the lights went out and daylight was not that far away, Moran's became such a place. One by one, without seeming to disturb any doors or windows Moran may have locked, the hunters of the night gathered. Men and women who hid in shadows and clothed themselves with darkness in their crusade against crime. This is where they met before assuming their civilian disguises, to spend some time with others like themselves. This was their brief chance to relax. By common assent, little business was discussed, maybe a warning here or a word there about which criminal was plotting what crime and who was seeking whom.

When did it start? Seamus Moran wondered as he watched a pint of his best seemingly disappear from the counter. When did the Dark Ones choose my place and why?

Those were two questions Moran could never answer. He could not remember a time when they did not gather, when spectral laughter was not heard every night after hours.

Maybe it's something like a family curse, was his thought as the flash of a fire opal drew his attention. He poured its owner another large Bushmill's then returned to his musing. My cousin Paddy has the same kind of crowd, less violent though. This sort would not be permitted in his place.

Thoughts of Paddy and his place uptown caused Moran to think of home. Not his apartment above the bar, but of that ancestral place from whence he and his came.

Moran was of the Gentry, the fair folk of Eire, that mythical land that was the Spirit of Ireland, a land that was currently in sore distress.

Moran had first thought to consult with Paddy, but the more he heard and the worse the news got, he knew that this was not his cousin's fight. If there was any truth to the tale, it was a killing matter, and the taking of life was something the elder Moran would not do.

Now these in here … Moran scanned the shadows of his bar, barely able to make out his costumed patrons … most of them have no qualms about pulling the trigger when it would do the most good. There were exceptions – the green one was a man of peace, the pink one killed when she had to but mostly avoided it. Otherwise these champions of justice were killers all.

Justice was what was needed – justice for his people, justice for his land. Maybe he could find it here.

Which one? Few of his after hour's patrons would believe that Moran was anything more than a short barkeep who served them drinks. They were men of cold steel and science, accepting only what they saw or could prove. To them ghosts were luminous paint and witches just deluded women. But there were those who knew differently.

"You look lost in thought, Seamus."

Such as the Nightmare, the man who just spoke.

"That I was, until yourself came along." Moran sighed, fully aware of what he was about to do. "Could I ask a favor?"

"If you want to peak under my mask, it'll cost you a drink."

"Maybe the next time, this is … can you stay after the rest have gone? It's … serious business, your kind of business."

"Look around, Seamus, they've already left. There's no one in place except you and me."

"How do they …"

"Trade secret."

Dawn was near. Michael Shaw, aka The Nightmare, sat unmasked in a booth waiting for Moran to bring breakfast. Over eggs, bacon and a cold glass of orange juice with which to welcome the morning, Moran made his plea.

"I hate like the devil to ask this of you, Michael."

"There's no harm in asking, Seamus. I can always say no."

"That you can, and after hearing what I have to say you probably will. If so, no hard feelings. You and your money will be welcome as long as there's a Moran's, however short a time that may be."

"Well, if there's a threat to my favorite watering hole I'm half convinced already. Now what's the problem?"

"Michael, there's trouble back home."

"So I've been reading."

"Not the Rebellion. That's a fight that's been going on for centuries and may go on for more. It's not Ireland I'm speaking of, it's Eire."

"They're not the same, I take it?"

Moran shook his head. "Every country has a physical plane – England, the United States, Ireland – and a spiritual plane – Albion, America and for Ireland, Eire. It is the soul of the Land, and Ireland's soul is blighted."

Shaw's eyes widened as his mind leaped. He sensed a revelation coming, one that would lead to new adventures and fresh challenges. "And you know this how?" he asked as he tried to repress a smile in what was a serious matter.

"It, Eire, is the land of my birth, the land I left when I came to America and the United States, the land to which I dream of one day returning."

Shaw lost his struggle as his smile broke free. "If you're from Eire, then given your size, that would make you a … leprechaun?"

"Close enough, Michael Shaw. And if it's my pot of gold you'll be asking about next, well, if you do this for me and make it back then you will have earned your chance at it. All I'll ask is a fair head start and if you catch me, it's yours."

"Seamus, I'll never spend the money I have. I don't do this," Shaw held up the mask of the Nightmare, "for the money. None of us do."

"Why do you do it?"

"Because, my friend, it must be done and we few are able and willing to do it. Now tell me, what ails your land and what must be done to save it?"

***

In another bar, some miles and many years away, two women met in a secluded booth. One was tall and dark and beautiful. The other was small, fair-skinned and while the man she loved thought of her as beautiful, she herself did not.

"I'm surprised he lets us in here," the smaller woman said, indicating the diminutive man behind the bar.

"It's not us Paddy objects to, Detective Jones, it's our methods. He thinks that there's always another way. If everyone believed that …"

"We wouldn't be needed. But tell me, why does the angel of vengeance need the help of a Baltimore cop?"

"You're much more than a Baltimore cop, Detective."

It was true. Despite her small size and slender build, Bianca Jones hunted monsters. Not just the two-legged kind that preyed on the weak and helpless – killers, rapists, drug dealers – but the terrors from dark places that saw humanity as cattle and play things. She was very good at what she did, but this skill was dearly earned and she was always aware of the dreadful cost of failure.

"Granted, but that doesn't answer my question. Why do you need me?"

"You accept who I am then. Few do."

Bianca smiled. "In Baltimore we do more than wait for monsters to come to us. We research and prepare. We want to be ready to meet a threat when it arises, not try to develop a plan while half the city is being destroyed. So yes, I've heard of you. Nemesis, goddess of retribution."

The woman in black returned the smile. "One of my many names, but it will do for now. As to why I need you …"

Nemesis drew several tattered pulp magazines from her bag and threw them on the table. They had the title FROM THE SHADOWS emblazoned across the top front and each garish cover featured a man dressed in black wielding oversized pistols while fighting some menace or the other. The captions at the bottom read "In this issue, another exciting adventure of The Nightmare."

Bianca picked up one of the books. "The Nightmare, I heard of him. A character like The Spider or The Pink Reaper."

"Would it surprise you to learn that he was real?"

"After what I seen, little surprises me. I assume there's a point to this?"

Nemesis gave little sign of hearing Bianca's question. "He was much like you, Michael was. No special powers, just an ordinary human doing extraordinary things. He too fought monsters and once helped bring down a god."

Bianca knew the look on Nemesis's face. She saw that look whenever her husband glanced her way. She felt it on her own face when she looked at him.

"You were in love with him."

"I still am and always will be. Yet he is in trouble and I cannot go to him."

Bianca looked at the date on one of the pulps. "If he was alive back then, by now he must be …"

The woman in black shook her head. "Where Michael is is beyond time and somehow closed to all those like me. That he could pass through shows that the way was not barred to mortals. Michael went to save a world but without help he will fail."

"All this time, is he still …."

"The realm of Eire is outside time. I have known of Michael's peril since he left this world. Unable to help him myself, I have waited long to find someone who could, a mortal like him who would dare challenge a god. If you are willing, I could send you to him. That, at least, is within my power."

"And so is bringing me back, I trust."

Nemesis nodded. "If you are successful. If not, there's little point."

Bianca sympathized with the woman across from her. To rescue a child she had stormed the gates of Hell. To save her love she had given up Heaven. But she was a practical woman.

"You're asking me to risk my life and leave the city I've sworn to defend unprotected just to save your old boyfriend. Why should I?"

"A fair question, Detective Jones. You just told me that you like to be ready to meet a threat when it develops. If, in the future, there comes a dire, desperate situation, would it not be a good thing to have the goddess of vengeance standing at your side?"

"Favor for favor, then?"

"It is the way of the worlds, Detective."

"Given the circumstances, call me 'Bianca.' And after you order us another round of drinks, you can explain just what I'm about to agree to."

* * *

The Nightmare stood alone in a dark, blasted landscape. Where there had once been green fields was nothing but brown earth. Burned stumps stood where trees had grown and houses were nothing but ruin and rubble.

There was no sign of life – human, animal or otherwise.

With a pistol in his right hand, the Nightmare carefully approached what had been a village. As he grew close he was met by the odors of decay, pestilence, of burned bodies and spilled blood. Not wanting to look, he searched what was left of the villagers' homes. He found what he had expected, signs of sickness and slaughter.

Some had died of a wasting illness, their lives slowly drawn from them, their emaciated bodies still lying in their beds. Other had died more quickly, slain by knife and sword. Still others had been set afire, their contorted, blackened bodies telling the Nightmare that they had been alive when fire was set to their flesh.

Seamus, thought the man in black, what have you gotten me into? At least I can't say you didn't warn me. His mind took him back to Moran's just after the bartender had asked his help.

"Those of us who have left Eire have always maintained a connection with it. We are of the Land and the Land is of us and there's no escaping that. It was a grand place and it was said the Lord made it so that a bit of heaven might be on Earth."

"If it was so grand, Seamus, why did you and your cousin leave it?"

"Aye, and a damned good question that is. I cannot speak for Paddy, that one has his own reasons for everything, but as for me, why does any boy leave a home where people love him and he has all he needs? For adventure, for the challenge, so that the boy might become a man. But if it's a good home you never really leave, do you? There's always a little piece inside you, to encourage you in the good times and comfort you in the bad."

Seamus tapped his chest. "Eire was always right here. And feeling it, knowing that it was but a door away, was enough for me. But now, Michael, that feeling is gone and there is a deep hole where once it was. Something bad has happened, but I do not know what."

"How can I help?"

"I can't go back, Michael, I've tried, but the door won't open for me nor for any of my kind. But for you, a noble man with a just cause, it might. You are not of the Land, so maybe it will not reject you as it did me. Find what's wrong. Stop it if you can. And if you cannot, if all is lost and the Soul of Ireland is gone then you must act as the avenger you are and kill the thing or things responsible. For if you do not, then once it has finished with my Land it will move on to others and one day find yours."

Shaw thought for a moment, then asked, "Seamus, in Eire, is there a god of sleep?"

"There are several, Angus for one, Epos Olloatir for another. Why?"

Shaw checked his guns, then put on the mask that covered one face and revealed another. "Pray to them if you can. Tell them the Nightmare is coming and he could use their help."

Seamus Moran then led the Nightmare to a back room of the bar where stood a door without a room.

"For two days it's been like this. Two days since I summoned it to try and go home. As I said, it will not open for me."

With a nod to the smaller man, the Nightmare strode to the portal and easily passed through it.

"To find myself here," the Nightmare said, again surveying the absolute destruction of the landscape and all who lived in it. A glow in the distance caught his attention. Dawn maybe? He waited and, when the sun did not rise to banish the seemingly eternal twilight, he walked toward the light, expecting to find the darkness that caused it.

***

I'm back in Hell, was Bianca's first thought when she saw where she was. Then she corrected herself. Hell, at least that part of Perdition where she had met and cheated the Devil, was not this bleak. Hell was where nothing grew except pain and where Hope did not exist. This land, this "Erie" as Nemesis had called it, had once been alive and what was left of the village in the distance told her that the people who lived there had had hope for the future.

Now, though, all growth had been stunted and all hope crushed.

"And I'm supposed to find one man, one dressed in black yet, in this wasteland."

Looking around, Bianca saw a glow in the distance. With nothing else to go on, she shouldered her pack and headed toward it.

***

As he approached his goal, the Nightmare was met first by some of the odors he had left in the ruined village. The smell of sickness and burning wafted his way. Then came the sounds of battle. No, battle was not the right word, for there was no clash of steel upon steel. It was the noise of slaughter – men crying out, women screaming, babies crying. Above it all was the sick laughter of those causing it as they gleefully went about their demon's work.

"If it's laughter they like," the Nightmare said to himself, "it's laughter they shall have."

Drawing his weapons, the man in black came close enough to pick out targets and unleashed his own brand of Hell.

At first the invaders of the village did not know what was among them. There was only the flash of lightning and the sound of thunder. Each time this occurred another of their comrades fell, a hole in his head or punched through his armor. He'd fall dead to the ground though there was no enemy close enough to strike him and no sign of spear or arrow.

Then they saw it, a figure all in black, the lightning spurting from his hands with thunder following. Whatever it was, it laughed as it killed, and like the banshee's mournful cry, the laughter promised death.

But these men were not the common criminals that the Nightmare was accustomed to fighting. Killers to a man and evil to their souls, they were warriors still. Once the initial shock wore off, they turned their attention away from the murder of innocents and focused on the threat at hand. They gathered then charged, each man trusting to his fate that he would not be the one to die next and praying to the god that sent him to be the one to strike down this specter.

This didn't work out as planned, thought the Nightmare. Though he fired as fast as he could, though with each shot another of foes dropped, those remaining came closer and closer. They'll be close soon and my guns will be useless except as clubs.

He thought of withdrawing, of fading back into the darkness of the night, but he was too close to the burning village, the light of the flames making that darkness too far away for him to reach before they caught him and hacked him to bits.

Better to die on his feet. Raising his guns he shot the two men closest to him. Then greeted the coming charge with a laugh of defiance.

***

Approaching the burning village, Bianca heard gunfire and laughter. From what Nemesis had told her, this meant the Nightmare was close by. A few minutes later she found him, in a fight for his life, firing his two .45s into a mass of warriors that kept getting closer no matter how many he shot down.

Guess the lady in black was right, Bianca thought as she came up from behind the crowd of men. He does need my help.

It was then the enormity of what she had to do struck her. So many. Bianca was no stranger to death. She had killed both men and monsters before but only once on this scale, the zombie war in New Orleans after Katrina. There, however, she had fought the undead. Here, in Eire, her foes were living men. That they had done terrible things made it easier, but not by much.

Placing her pack on the ground, Bianca removed from two small, round objects. Knowing this day would be relived in dreams for years to come, she pulled the pins on the grenades and threw them into the crowd just as it started its charge.

Twin explosions shook the ground and blew the men closest to them into pieces. They also startled the rest to the point where the black ghost that had killed so many of them was for the moment forgotten.

Some turned to see a small, slender woman standing behind them. She was not laughing and the look on her face was unmistakable. Some sorrow and regret but mostly determination. She meant to kill them. Seeing that she held only what looked like a hollow tube, the men rushed her.

None got close enough to pose a threat. Bianca's Mossberg shotgun roared, its flechette loads tearing her attackers into pieces. Again and again she let loose tiny slivers of death and with each shot her foes fell. And when the Nightmare added his withering fire, the spirit of the warriors broke and they ran like cowards into the night, leaving the two crime fighters alone on the field of battle.

Wading through the blood and gore of the dead, the Nightmare greeted Bianca with, "Thanks. Seamus didn't tell me that he was sending reinforcements." He held out his hand. "I'm called …"

"The Nightmare, I know, aka Michael Shaw, one of the masked vigilantes of the thirties. Later … well, I better not say. I'm Bianca Jones, Detective Sergeant with the Baltimore Police Department. And whoever this Seamus is, he didn't send me."

"Miss Jones, or rather, Sergeant Jones. Let's see. You're a woman police sergeant, carrying a kind of shotgun I've never seen. Your clothing is not the kind that women of my era would wear and you seem to know all about me. So if Seamus didn't send you, who did and from how far into the future have you come?"

"The when doesn't matter and as for who, Leda sends her love."

That name. The name by which Michael Shaw knew and loved Nemesis. There had been evenings of bloodshed and vengeance and one marvelous night of passion. Later, after he had given his life for her and she had brought him back from the very brink of death they had separately faced down and beaten a god. She was his first true love and before this night he had had no hope of ever seeing her again.

"Leda sent you. Does that mean that in your time we …"

Bianca shook her head. "What will be, what Fate allows, I can't reveal. But let me ask you this – what the hell were you thinking, taking on a village of crazed men with sharp weapons?"

The Nightmare shrugged. "It seemed like a good idea at the time. Back … where I come from I laugh and start shooting. Some fight back and die, the rest run away." He looked at the bodies on the ground. "These didn't run."

"That because they're not pulp fiction gangsters who are afraid to die. These are warriors to whom death in battle is a glorious thing. Remember that the next time we face them. And please take off that mask when I'm talking to you. It's like talking to a shadow."

Thinking, He doesn't wear a mask, the Nightmare tried to remove his, and failed.

"It won't come off."

"Odd." Like the Nightmare had only a short while ago, Bianca looked at the lifeless bodies around them. "You killed a lot of men today. How many times did you reload those cannons?"

It was then that the Nightmare realized that he had not stopped to reload. "I didn't."

"And how many round do those guns carry?"

Again looking at the dead, the Nightmare replied, "Not that many."

"Strange forces are at work here, Michael. Look at the dead."

He did. Not all appeared to have come from the Land. Many races were represented, some of them not native to the Earth they knew.

"God!" the Nightmare exclaimed.

"More than one, Michael. Let's hope some of them are on our side. Now to find out what's going on in this place."

* * *

Thanks to the intervention of the two mortal fighters, this time there were survivors. All had hidden in what had been vain hopes that maybe they would be spared, maybe the killers would not find them, that maybe death would pass them by. Bianca wanted to seek them out.

"No," cautioned the Nightmare, "They're frightened and who knows what they might do if two blood-stained killers sought them out. We'll stand here, weapons away, and let them come to us."

They stood and waited, the tall man in black whose very appearance marked him as a creature of the night and the small woman whose duty it was to mete out justice and vengeance. Slowly, as the residents realized that the screaming and crying had ceased and silence once more ruled their village they began to emerge from their hiding holes.

A strange lot they were, the stuff of myth and legends. Leprechauns like Seamus and his cousin, creatures smaller still who flew on paper-thin wings, beasts who could have torn unarmed men apart but who were no match for trained soldiers. Most appeared human, but there was something about them that hinted that they possibly were something more, or maybe something less.

There were twenty in all, twenty survivors in a village where maybe ten times that number once lived. As they emerged from hiding Bianca and the Nightmare saw that despite their size, appearance or nature they were united in one thing, they were all scared.

As they gathered on the main street it was not long before they noticed the pair. Some fled back into hiding. Others, noting that the newcomers had not attacked, waited. A few, seeing blood on the clothing of the two but no wounds on their bodies, counted the dead behind them, breathed a sigh a relief and said a silent prayer of thanks. One of these few approached.

He was a child-sized creature, smaller than Bianca. As he came nearer his age became evident – graying hair, a lined face, and eyes that had seen too much of life.

"You did this?"

The Nightmare nodded as Bianca answered, "Yes."

What would have been a smile under happier circumstances creased the elder's face. "Then the Mother Goddess heard our pleas. We did not think any of the Fair Ones left." He looked around, as if searching for something. "Where is your army?"

"We do not need an army," The Nightmare replied in what he called his "spooky voice."

"All this? The two of you alone did … this?" Fear and awe was in the old man's voice. He dared to ask. "What are you?"

Bianca would have replied that they were just two people from another land sent to help. The Nightmare had a better sense of the dramatic.

"We are Retribution and Justice. We are Vengeance and Nightmare. We were sent to restore this land."

"Angus, Epos, Arian," whispered the elder as he wondered.

Knowing what it might mean to be named in a magical land, Bianca said firmly, "We are none of these. Our names are our own. And not for you to know. If you must, call us Bán and Tromluí."

The man nodded. "And I am Liam. Your names will be remembered as long as this village stands. You saved us. How may we serve you?"

The cop in Bianca took over. "Tell us what happened. When did the trouble start?"

"When has there not been trouble in Eire? Always there has been war and disease. But nothing like this. Plague and destruction have ravaged all the Land. First the pestilence comes. It kills some and weakens the rest. Then a blight steals the crops away. Sick and hungry, we are no match for the killers that come to finish the job."

"You said all the Land. How do you know this?"

Liam held his hand palm out. A small blue shape fluttered into it. "The piskies spread the news that all of Eire is besieged with warriors destroying all as they march to the sea."

"Thank you, Liam. Excuse us a moment. Tromluí and I must confer." The elder withdrew.

"What's this 'Tromluí and Bán?'"

"Irish for nightmare and white. Seemed a better idea than taking on the names and attributes of local gods, although that may be too late after your 'Retribution and Justice' pronouncement."

"I was just …"

"I know what you were doing, Michael. In our world it's dramatic and effective. But in a realm like this, words are magic."

"With just the two of against an army, I'll take all the help we can get. How soon do you think those marauders will be back?"

"Once they'll regroup, soon enough. They may wait for some sorcerous help."

"Then we'd best get ready for them."

It hurt her to say it. "Michael, we'd best get going before they do."

"What, but when those killers come back …"

"If we fight to save the village, we'll lose the Land. To save the Land …"

"We let the village die."

It was the logical thing to do, the man who was The Nightmare admitted to himself but that was no comfort at all. He would have argued with Bianca but his companion had waved Liam back.

"The heart of Eire," she asked the elder, "where is it?"

He pointed northeast. "Temair, where stands the Stone of Destiny, where lies the entrance to the otherworld. A day's journey, maybe more. You are going there?"

"Yes," Bianca admitted. "We do not know if this evil began or will end there, but that is where it might be stopped."

There was sadness in the old man's eyes and understanding in his voice as he asked, "And what of us?"

Pointing to the field of fallen men Bianca replied, "There are weapons out there. You can use them to fight and die." Then she pointed to the hills and forest behind the village. "Or you can hide and maybe live."

"A poor choice, Lady Bán."

"Your only one, Liam." To the Nightmare, Bianca said, "Let's go."

"Shouldn't we stop to eat and sleep?'

"Are you tired or hungry? I'm not."

"Neither am I, but I should be."

"Spirits at work again," Bianca said in disgust. "Come on, let's kill some gods."

***

They had been walking north for most of an hour when the Nightmare asked, "Why are we going to this Temair?"

"It's a place to start. If it is the heart of Eire, whoever's behind this either started there, in which case we may find a trail or is heading there, in which case we'll wait for him."

"What if he's still there?"

"Then we sit down with him and calmly discuss why he turned a paradise into a wasteland and ask him politely to make things right again. Either that or just kill him."

"I think we'd best kill him."

Later, after they had trekked more than half a day, "This land is barren," Bianca observed, "withered crops, burned villages, no life at all. Given what we left, I think the raiders came this way."

"I agree." After studying his surroundings the Nightmare added, "Reminds me of the Great War."

"You fought in World War I?" As soon as she spoke, Bianca realized her mistake.

The Nightmare nodded solemnly. "So there's going to be another one? Don't worry; your news isn't a surprise to anyone paying attention. It's always been a question of when, not if. I don't suppose you'd like to tell me?"

Bianca shook her head. "I've said too much already."

"At least tell me if we win."

"The good guys always do, don't they."

"We usually do, at least so far."

Bianca suddenly realized that she had the power to change history. Should I tell him, she wondered. Tell him about Germany and the Final

Solution, Stalin and the Iron Curtain, Pearl Harbor and the Atomic Bomb? He's a hero. He could gather the others and together they could kill Hitler and prevent the Third Reich. There might still be war but it might not be as bad. Or it might be worse.

That was the trouble with power. Using it may not always be the best course of action. Bianca decided to leave well enough alone.

That led her to consider her presence in Eire. Was what they were doing there the best course of action? Maybe the Land was supposed to die so that a better one might be reborn. Maybe their intervention …

Enough, she yelled at herself, You're thinking too much. Just do the job you came to do and get out of this hell.

Hell. If the desolation around them reminded Shaw of the war, it reminded Bianca of the Plains outside Hell. She and her partner had gone there to rescue an innocent. The journey had forced her to face the worst parts of herself. With help she overcame them and left them on the sands of Perdition.

Now Bianca found herself on a similar journey. Walking with a partner through a mythical land. They did not tire, they were not hungry and their guns did not empty. Magic was working. Maybe they should use it.

"Michael."

"Yes?"

"When the time comes to fight, before you act, before you even draw your guns, tell yourself to become Nightmare."

"I am the Nightmare."

"Not the Nightmare, just Nightmare, the terror of dreams brought to life."

"This has something to do with what you said before, about words and names having power."

"It has everything to do with it."

"Worth a try. But if I'm to be Tromluí in fact as well as name, what of Bán?"

"She becomes Vengeance."

***

It could have been the same day, maybe the next. In a sunless world there were no days or hours and time was merely an illusion.

"Are we there yet?"

"Tired, Michael?"

"Bored."

"Well, if that slight glow on what I think might be the horizon mean anything, you won't be bored for long."

"Then we should start making plans for when we … wait. What was that?"

"I didn't hear anyth…"

"You wouldn't. Back on Earth I worked and fought in the shadows. I was part of the night. Here it's as if the darkness is a part of me. There is something out there."

Bianca began to bring up her gun.

"No, don't. Gunfire will only attract attention. Let me handle this. You just keep talking."

Bianca turned to ask, "About what?" but the Nightmare was gone.

There was not much cover in the wasted land of Eire – broken stone fences, husks of trees, partly collapsed walls, but what there was was sufficient to hide a small band of men. Somehow the Nightmare knew where each of them was.

Miss Jones was right, he thought. We are close. This must be the first outpost. He sensed movement in the night then felt one of the lookouts leaving his post, no doubt to spread word about the intruders.

Can't have that. Suddenly he was flowing through the darkness, travelling faster than he ever could in the mortal plane. There was no conscious thought in this, just a desire to catch the running man. When he did, he used a knife he'd taken from one of his foes from the village to silence the man forever.

There are six others. How he knew this he could not say but reaching through the night he found them, flowed to them and used his knife to end their threat. Then he was back with Bianca.

When he again appeared at her side the detective tried not to appear startled. She almost asked how things had gone then saw his cleaning blood off a wicked looking knife.

"There'll be no warning from this direction," said the Nightmare casually, as of the deaths of seven men had not affected him. "Here."

He handed Bianca a pair of matched blades – long knives, short swords – Bianca wasn't sure. "I don't need these."

"Maybe Bianca Jones doesn't, but Bán soon will. In a crowd guns are of little use except as clubs. These are best for close quarter fighting."

"And how do you know they're be close quarter fighting?"

"To quote one of my colleagues, I know."

The pair had not gone much further when distant noises reached them. The Nightmare knew those sounds from the war, they were the sounds of encamped men.

Stealthily they approached, Bianca following the Nightmare, matching him step for step, moving when he did and stopping when he stopped. Finally they reached the camp.

As the Nightmare called on the night to hide them, the pair surveyed the scene.

"Fifty, maybe seventy-five men," the experienced soldier explained to the detective. "Nothing permanent. Those tents are made to be taken down quickly. Look there." The Nightmare indicated one side of the camp. "Men preparing to leave."

"And there," Bianca drew his attention to the other side, "more men coming in. But from where?"

"Up there, maybe?"

The Nightmare pointed past the far side of the camp to where stood a castle. Temair, the Heart of the Land. It was not the fairy tale palace one reads about in stories. Instead it was a stone fortress, one that appeared easy to defend and difficult to breach.

"Liam said that Temair was a gateway to other worlds."

"From which, Miss Jones, whoever or whatever's behind this may be bringing in troops. We have to get in there."

"Any suggestions, other than knocking on the front door and asking to come in."

"I've gotten into more formidable places. But first we have to get past these men."

"Why not just go around them?'

"That would be my first choice, Miss Jones, except ..." The Nightmare pointed at the camp. Men were gathering their weapons and coming towards them. "I think someone knows we're here. We'll have to go through them."

As the Nightmare drew his .45s Bianca readied her shotgun, made sure her .40 caliber pistol was close to hand. "We'll use out guns until they get close," she said.

"And then?"

"Then we let Tromluí and Bán take over. Start us off, Michael."

"Why not?"

The Nightmare laughed and the pair opened fire.

***

The order came from the castle. There were intruders approaching from the south. They were to be stopped at all costs.

As the men and those who walked like men gathered, they saw two figures at the edge of the woods, a tall one in black and a youth. Neither was armored. Nor did they appear to be carrying any weapons. This won't be much of a fight, most of them thought.

Then there was laughter and thunder and death came for no reason and the men knew them for what they were – wizards or gods. No matter, they were warriors and had their orders. And whatever their nature, the pair would die.

The men rushed forward only to be felled by the Nightmare's bullets or ripped to shreds by Bianca's flechette loads. Still they came, grinning in the face of almost certain death. They knew, or thought they knew, that the pair could not stop them all and sooner rather than later they would be within spear's point or sword's edge and that would be the end of them.

Bianca and the Nightmare knew this as well. As their targets came closer they killed more of them but before they got too close, Bianca said, "Now would be the time, Michael."

"Agreed, and let's pray you're right."

As they surrendered to their other selves the screaming began.

The two at the woods, the ones that were expected to die easy and messy deaths were suddenly not there. Instead each man faced that which frightened him the most, the things that haunted his dreams and caused him to wake screaming from sleep. Some broke and ran, others stood paralyzed with fright. Still others collapsed in fear.

The man who had been the Nightmare and who was now Tromluí felt their fears and fed on them. Growing stronger, he sent his night terrors further outward, engulfing those still in camp, bringing them to their knees to weep like children.

But there are men who do not fear, or if they do have the strength to overcome it. Horrible monsters, terrible beasts, skinless hags with diseased flesh have no power over them for they have caused more suffering than could ever be dreamt and had enjoyed doing so. And there were such men among those advancing, men unaffected by what seemed to be a wizard's curse.

It was these men that caused she who was now Bán to draw her blades and go among them. Against her speed and skill these men had no chance and one by one were cut down. And when none stood against her Bán went down into the camp and continued her bloody work.

When it was over, when there was nothing left but dead men and empty tents, Bianca and Nightmare slowly came back to themselves.

Bianca looked over the slaughter. "What have we done?"

"What we had to do."

"I'm not so sure. There must have been a better way." She looked down at her hands and he blades they held. Both were bloody. She would have thrown the weapons down had she been sure she would not need them again.

"What have we become?" she asked.

"Something more."

"You enjoyed doing this?" With a wave of her red stained hand Bianca indicated the dead and moaning.

"Not exactly, but … look at how I dress, what I do, how I do it. It would be easier to strike fear into the hearts of evildoers if I could, well, actually strike fear."

"At what cost? Your life, your mind, your soul. How much of Michael Shaw would Tromluí allow to remain, and what if he chose not to stop with the hearts of bad guys? Magic has a price, Michael, just look around you to know what it costs."

Again Bianca looked at her hands. This time she did drop her blades.

"Point taken, but if we don't want to pay another installment we better get up to the castle before whoever sends down more men."

"You start for Temair, I'm going to search out this gateway to the otherworld."

"Leaving so soon? The party's not over."

"Not yet, maybe not ever, but as you said, we do what we have to do."

As Bianca walked away, the Nightmare could not help but think of how much she reminded him of someone else, although Leda would not have left her weapons, nor would she have thought about the cost of using them.

***

The entrance to the otherworlds. That's what Liam had called it back at the village. If it truly was, it might be her way back, possibly her only way back. That's not why Bianca sought it but it was how she was going to find it. Resisting the impulse to click her heels together she began repeating, "There's no place like home, there's no place like home."

She felt a tug, one which led her to the east of Castle Temair. There she found a mound of earth about the size of a hill, a round hole at its base. Through the hole Bianca sensed Baltimore, her husband Joe and the 21st century. No troops were coming from it, but how long would that last? She did what she had to do. Then, saying goodbye to all she knew and loved, she went to join the Nightmare.

***

The approach to Temair was guarded, but not well. To one whose practice it was to blend with the shadows it was an easy task in this endless twilight for the Nightmare to avoid the guards.

"But why blend with the shadows when you can become them?" asked a voice inside his head, a voice he knew to be Tromluí's. But Tromluí was a part of him, was he not?

"Think, Michael, how easy it would be to slide from one shadow to the next, no fear of detection. Where there was darkness and light, there you would be, striking down your enemies, teaching them the true meaning of fear."

At what cost? the Nightmare wondered, thinking back on Bianca's warning. My life, my soul, myself?

Somehow the Nightmare knew that it was not a part of himself that answered. "You need not worry, Michael, I want nothing from you, only the fear of others."

"What have we done?" he echoed Bianca. "What have we created?" Whatever it was, it was not something he could take home with him, nor did he want it inside him.

"While I appreciate the offer, I think I'll pass." He drew his guns, checked their loads. "I'll make do with these."

Tromluí would have protested but as its creator, the Nightmare was able to push it away and out of his conscious mind.

He was now at the castle gates. Ahead of him was the courtyard and next the Great Hall. The Nightmare suspected that that was where he'd find the source of the Land's troubles.

"Well, Michael," he said aloud to himself, "it's just you, your guns and a laugh against who knows what. The way it should be, without the hocus-pocus. Time to play."

And with that he marched toward the Great Hall to face who knows what.

The first thing that hit him was a wave of nausea. He fought back the urge to vomit then struggled not to soil his trousers. His skin grew clammy then hot as a fever threatened to take him. An itchy rash began in places he did not want to think about.

Disease, he knew, was the first to plague the villages. But his symptoms were not plague-like, merely annoying and potentially embarrassing. His maladies did however tell him that he was in the right place.

Then he saw her, a diseased-ridden hag with more sores than skin. Lesions on her body oozed pus when they did not leak blood. She smelled of putrescence and decay. On seeing her, the Nightmare was glad that he could kill from a distance, for he had no wish to get any nearer to the creature than he must.

"Madame," he said politely, "I think it's past time that you saw a physician."

What was probably a cackle came out as a death rattle followed by a prolonged cough. "I doubt if any would heal me, young man. I am the reason for their profession and the source of their wealth. I am Cailleach, and I am Sickness Herself."

Leveling a .45 in her direction, the Nightmare said, "And I have a cure for that sickness."

The diseased goddess laughed again, phlegm gurgling in her throat as she did. "You would think to kill a god? Destroy this form and I will find another."

"And in the meantime the Land will have a chance to heal."

Cailleach smiled, if a show of bleeding gums and blackened teeth could be called a smile. "So be it," she said and when the Nightmare fired she made no move to avoid her fate.

He shot her twice, in her head and heart. As she collapsed and began to decay, the Nightmare thought he heard her say, "Beware the stranger and your other self."

Before the Nightmare could consider these words he heard,

"He told us you would come. Where is your other?"

Turning, the Nightmare saw a man at the far end of the hall. He was armored. A sheathed sword hung at his side and in his hands were a shield and spear. The man was tall and well-muscled, the image of the perfect warrior.

"You must be War."

The man shrugged. "War, Death, Destruction – it's all the same is it not?"

"Who are you and why do you plague this land?"

"I am called Elphane by some and as for plagues, they were Cailleach's doing. I brought war and destruction. As for why …" It seemed to the Nightmare as if the warrior god had tried to speak but could not. He did, however, turn and look at the doorway behind him.

Pistols in hand, the Nightmare advanced, expecting Elphane's attack at any time.

"Were we to fight, dark one," cautioned the god, "you would lose."

"Were I to fire these, you would die."

At this Elphane smiled. "I can throw this spear faster than a man can blink and it always flies true. My shield is such that nothing can pierce it, indeed, whatever force strikes it is returned threefold against my attacker. And when I draw my sword it cuts so clean that you will not feel your head leave your neck. As I said, dark one, were we to fight you would lose."

Bizarre plans ran through the Nightmare's mind. Could he catch the spear? Could he fire and not hit the shield? If his bullets did strike the shield could he then run in front of the god so that they struck him? Rejecting these ideas he simply asked,

"And if we do not fight?"

"Then how could you lose?"

Nodding in understanding, the man in black holstered his .45s. As he approached the far doorway of the Great Hall Elphane stepped aside. To the Nightmare's questioning glance he replied, "I am the god of death and destruction, not a porter. Enter of your own free will. Beware the stranger and your other self."

That phrase again. Who was the stranger? Was it the "he" who had warned Elphane of his coming? And was his other self Tromluí or could it be Miss Jones? What had become of her and would she somehow betray him?

The room which the Nightmare entered was smaller than the Great Hall and was empty of all but a chair and the man sitting in it. If man he was. He was dressed in white and shone with an inner brightness that made the torches on the walls unnecessary. There had been boredom on his face when the Nightmare came in but that disappeared when he saw the man in black.

Immediately sensing that this being was the one responsible for the troubles plaguing the Land, the Nightmare decided not to waste time. Drawing his .45s he fired but as he did so a shadow rose up before the shining man and seemingly swallowed the bullets.

"You didn't think it would be that easy, did you?" the man asked. "Meet your other self."

At the man's words the Nightmare knew the shadow creature for what it was. It was Tromluí, that part of him that he had rejected.

"You came to this Land to stop me and to stop me you took part of the Land into yourself. And when you rejected it you not only gave me the means to stop you but to use that part of you to enter your world when I am done ravaging this one."

From outside the castle there came the sound of thunder and from the doorway the voice of Bianca Jones.

"Your gateway to other worlds just collapsed." To the Nightmare she explained, "Several grenades going off at one will do that to a hole in a hill. We're probably trapped in this world, but then again, so is he."

As Bianca spoke, the Nightmare noticed that she carried a spear in one hand and a sword in the other. "How did you get those?"

"I'll explain later. In the meantime, who's our new best friend?"

"Fools. You are in the presence of Apollonius of Tyana, the true Messiah over that Nazarene pretender. Long have I wandered the many planes of existence, looking for a world such as this, one whose mortal plane is so beset with strife that I can usurp its very gods and cause them to do my bidding. Know this, I needed that gateway only to bring in warriors with which to overwhelm this land. There are other paths which I may trod. Your souls for one."

And the shade of Bán rose up next to that of Tromluí.

"Your own selves will devour you and through them will I gain access to your world."

As the two spirits began to advance Bianca turned to the Nightmare.

"Trade you," she suggested and at his hesitation added, "Trust me."

Seeing no other choice, he agreed.

Tromluí which was Nightmare itself enveloped Bianca, filling her being with horrors which would have overwhelmed anyone else. But these terrors paled in comparison to those which the detective has faced in real life. She was a Baltimore City cop and had seen it all – men gunned down for no reason, women brutalized beyond belief, children raped and murdered. Bianca had fought monsters and had walked the plains of Hell.

Nothing scared her anymore save the possibility that she would one day fail the people and the city she loved. And since she had lived that fear every day for the past few years, experiencing it again had little effect on her. Powerless over her, Tromluí faded away

As the Nightmare faced Bán he remembered what she as part of Bianca had done to the soldiers outside the castle. And in remembering, smiled. Now and then he saw in this spirit of vengeance an aspect of Nemesis, the goddess and woman whom he loved. Whispering softly the name "Leda" he let that love shine through. And as Bán had been born of Bianca, and Bianca had been sent by Nemesis, the spirit felt the love. With no vengeance to take, Bán faded.

"Is that all you got?" Bianca asked. Saying "catch" she tossed the sword to the Nightmare.

"Fools," Apollonius said again and unleashed his powers against them. Heat seared one, cold froze the other. They would have fallen, should have fallen but their belief in themselves was stronger than any self-named god. Her skin blistering, Bianca drew back her arm. Barely able to feel his limbs, the Nightmare advanced with his sword.

Bianca let loose the spear that always flew true. It pinned the would-be messiah to his chair. The Nightmare moved closer. One swing and Apollonius did not even feel his head leave his neck.

"Did we win?" asked a very frostbitten Nightmare. Feeling in his fingers and toes was gone and it felt as if his arms and legs were next.

"If the bad guy's dead I think so," answered Bianca, her every nerve ending screaming in pain, "but right now it doesn't feel like it."

"F-fire and ice," said the Nightmare through shivering lips. "We're in a magical realm. Do you think …"

"Worth a shot. It's that or die."

Crawling over to each other, they just managed to embrace before losing consciousness.

***

It was hours, or maybe just minutes later, when they awoke. Both were seemingly healed, the Nightmare with some small tingling in his fingers and Bianca with a decent tan for the first and only time in her life.

The headless body of Apollonius was still in its chair but, like their pain, was beginning to fade.

"That's never a good sign," Bianca said.

"Like us, he was a stranger to the Land. Now we have to find our way back. Any ideas?"

Before she could answer, Elphane came into the room. "May I have my weapons back now?"

"That reminds me, Miss Jones, you never did explain how you got them."

"It seems that there are two answers to my riddle. One was not to fight and the other ..."

"While he was bragging about his weapons I kicked him in the balls and took what I needed," Bianca explained.

"Of the two, I liked your answer better, dark one." Elphane looked at what remained of the corpse. "Still, you managed to free the Land from the stranger and for that you have my thanks."

"And mine as well, Michael."

At the sound of a familiar voice the Nightmare looked around to see a smaller than average man.

"Seamus, but I thought ..."

"With that one gone," Seamus indicated the now almost vanished body of Apollonius, "the way once again opened, my way at least. I understand it will take some digging to repair this lady's handiwork." He turned to Bianca. "Seamus Moran, my lady, at your service. And may I say it's nice to meet a lady of the proper height for once."

Taking the proffered hand, Bianca said, "I've met your cousin."

"Then you know that good looks run in the family. That is, they run from Paddy and run to me. Ready to go back, Michael?"

"Wait, what of the Land, what of Eire? How will it heal itself?"

"Rest assured, my lady, the one thing we have is plenty of fertility gods and goddesses. The Land will heal amid much pleasure. Michael, it's time I saw you home."

"Past time, I'd say, Seamus, but what of Miss Jones?"

"She'd be more than welcome. She'd fit in well with your group. But hers is a different path. And now if you're ready?"

"A moment, Seamus. Miss Jones, thank you for your help. It was a pleasure fighting at your side."

"Likewise, Michael."

"Give Leda my love. Maybe one day ..."

"Maybe. One never knows. Goodbye, Michael."

"Goodbye, Miss Jones."

***

In a New York tavern, many years away, two women again met in a secluded booth.

"He's safe then," asked a woman in black.

"As safe as anyone who does what he does. And from what I've read …"

"One never knows, Bianca. The past at times is as fluid as the future. But for now he's safe back then. And I owe you."

"Damn straight you do. I just pray I never have to call in the debt."

A smallish man who looked very much like his cousin came over to their table. "Excuse me, ladies."

"Yes, Paddy?"

"Many, many years ago a man dressed in black with a wicked laugh came to me at closing time and begged a favor. He asked that if two deadly and beautiful women should ever come twice to my bar I was to give them these," he handed them sealed envelopes, "and serve them this."

Paddy filled their glasses from a bottle that was old when he was young and the Irish had first learned what to do with the juice of the barley. "Drinks tonight are on Michael Shaw."

Bianca's message was simply "With all my thanks."

Nemesis's message was simply "With all my love."

And for that moment and many more, the laugh of the Nightmare echoed in their minds.

THE FIRST WISH

"Let's just stop in for a minute," Mitzi Patton told her friend Hester Workman. "I want to show you what I bought. There's this darling little statue of a squirrel that would be just right for … what's that?"

They heard the sounds as soon as they came through the door, two voices – one moaning, one sighing, one female, one male. Added to the noise of creaking bedsprings, it was clear what was going on upstairs.

"I had better go." Hester started to back out the door. Mitzi grabbed her arm.

"No, stay. I might … need a witness."

Slowly, quietly, the two women ascended the stairs. With her friend behind her, Mitzi entered the bedroom.

"What the hell is going on in here?"

The answer to that question was quite clear. Mitzi's husband Tony was naked and so was the woman in bed with him.

No, not a woman, a young girl. One of the neighborhood children.

"Jana Bell, is that you?"

"I'm sorry, Mrs. Patton." There was fear and shame and anguish in the girl's cry as she looked first at Mitzi then at Patton then back again. "He … he forced me to." She quickly gathered her clothes and ran from the room.

Naked, Patton got out of bed. "I can explain," he said.

"No, you can't." There was disgust and loathing in Mitzi's voice. "Get dressed, you sick bastard, or go to jail naked." She and Hester turned, leaving Patton alone.

The police came. Evidence was collected from the house. Patton was taken into custody and samples taken from his body. All that was left was to contact the victim and her family, get a statement and file the charges.

Except Jana Bell denied anything had happened. She had been home alone all day working on a report for school and socializing with her friends on the Internet.

An examination of her computer bore this out. A medical examination by a forensic nurse at City of Hope Hospital confirmed that Jana's body bore no sign of physical or sexual assault. With apologies to Jana and her family Detective Mike Erickson went back to Patton's house.

"But we saw her with him."

Erickson nodded in understanding. "I'm sure you and Ms. Workman did, or thought so. And you did the right thing by calling us."

"But I was so sure."

The detective offered the only possible explanation. "Some men, when they become obsessed with something they can't have will use a look-alike as a … substitute. Could your husband …"

"A hooker! That son of a bitch brought a hooker into my house!" Suddenly Mitzi stopped her shouting and looked puzzled. "But how would a whore know my name? Why would she apologize?"

These were questions Erickson was asking himself. He had a definite crime with two witnesses, but the girl in question had not been assaulted.

"Maybe," Erickson suggested as he himself was looking for an explanation, "that was part of your husband's game, getting caught and all. Some men get excited by shame and humiliation."

Mitzi shook her head. "Not Tony, not his shame anyway."

Erickson had one more question. "This is a delicate matter, but outside of, um, normal relations, did your husband have any peculiar preference or fetishes?"

Mitzi thought of some of things he had forced her to do, things no decent woman should have to endure. Things that were none of this detective's business.

"I couldn't say. I do know that he spent a lot of time on his computer, too much time if you know what I mean. And lately, he hasn't been … as demanding."

"We have his computer and we're getting a warrant to search it. If we find anything on it …" Erickson trailed off and readied himself to deliver the bad news.

"I know what you saw, Mrs. Patton, and I believe that you saw it. But there's no evidence that Jana Bell was assaulted in any way. Without her or another complaining victim, we have no cause to hold your husband."

"You're setting him free! You're sending him … back here! To this house, to my house? No, you can't do that."

"We have nothing to hold him on. Now there are civil options …."

"To Hell with that. I want that pervert locked away. He was with a hooker, isn't consorting with a whore against the law?"

"A misdemeanor, yes, but we have no evidence that this woman, this girl, whoever she was, was a prostitute. I'm sorry."

It wasn't just talk. As he left the Pattons' home, Erickson was sorry. Every part of him that was a cop knew something bad had happened in that house and that something bad was likely to happen again. But under the law there was nothing he could do. He decided to rush the warrant on Patton's computer and hope to find something nasty and illegal.

Two days later, Jana Bell did not come home from school. It was early evening when her naked and savaged body was found in a park near her home. This time there were doubts, no questions. Before she was killed, Jana had been sexually assaulted in every way possible.

A warrant was served on the Pattons' house. When a pair of panties believed to have been worn by Jana was found under a cushion of his basement couch, Tony Patton was arrested and charged with her murder. As he was being led away, homicide detective Bethany Steele saw Mitzi Patton smiling. It was not, she thought, a smile of relief but one of having accomplished a great thing. It briefly bothered her, but at the time Beth was more bothered by the things that had been done to the girl and so she put it out of her mind.

***

Some months later, other aspects of the case began to bother Beth.

"It doesn't make sense," she said to her friend and sometime partner Bianca Jones.

"Very little about child murders makes sense, Beth. That's why I'm sometimes glad I can kill my monsters when I catch them. What's the problem?"

Before answering, Beth looked at the two empty glasses in front of her and signaled the waiter. Frank's Hall was a cop bar, so there was no worry about discussing the case in a public place. Still, she lowered her voice before answering.

"Things don't add up. Mitzi Patton and Hester Workman both swear that the girl looked and sounded like Jana. And the girl seemed to have recognized the wife."

"But it wasn't her?"

"No physical evidence that it was. Mrs. Patton said she saw blood on him and the sheets. He washed his blood off and the blood from the sheets …"

"Not a match for Jana?"

Beth shook her head. "It's not blood. It's not … anything. The lab's tried everything; all the tests came back negative. The girl's body was abused in the most horrible way, but again – nothing. No hairs, no fibers, no blood or DNA from the killer. The only real evidence we have against Patton are the panties we found under his couch."

"Used?"

"Definitely worn, but there wasn't enough on them to say by whom."

"No, Beth, I meant used by Patton."

"You mean … ewwww, but no."

"So Patton can claim they were planted. By now his lawyer's probably bought a similar pair from every shop in Baltimore. What about the rape kits and Jana's fingernails, any evidence there?"

"There's something there but who knows what. Again, all tests are negative."

"Usually, two negatives make a positive. Have the lab compare the stuff from the sheets to the stuff from Jana."

"Bianca, when you compare nothing to nothing, you usually get nothing."

"Have Tammy do it. Tell her to use some of the techniques she learned from Joe."

Tammy Dolan was a BPD Criminalist who sometimes assisted Bianca in cases that involved the strange, the weird or the supernatural. Joe Russo was Bianca's husband, drawn into the world of fighting inhuman monsters by his love for her. He owned a bookstore whose back room was filled tomes and grimoires of ancient lore and magic.

"You think this could be one of … those cases?"

"If you mean one of my cases, God I hope not. I've got enough to handle right now. Remember that house in the Southwest District that disappeared?"

"I've heard about the screams in the night from the vacant lot."

"That's the one. The house came back with seven dead inside, none of whom were in it when it vanished. Tavon's Quick Response Team has it surrounded with instructions to capture anyone or kill anything that tries to leave."

The waiter came by with another round. Again, Beth insisted on paying. That told Bianca all she needed to know. "What do you want, Beth?"

Bethany Steele looked across the table at her friend and thought, not for the first time, that Bianca didn't look like a cop.

It was true. Bianca Jones was barely five foot tall with a slim build and features that made her look years younger than her age. She did not look like someone who had faced down beasts and monsters most people would deny were real. Beth had worked on some of those cases, but it was always Bianca who had taken point, who faced the worst of it on her own. It was Bianca who, on a regular basis, put her life and sometimes her soul at risk as part of her job.

"We need Patton to talk. To explain the panties, to tell us about the girl his wife saw him with, to … hell, to help us make sense of it all. Without some sort of explanation, he might walk."

Bianca nodded in understanding, but added, "Possible, but I doubt it. The jury will hear about what happened in his bedroom. They'll hear about the panties, and his attraction for very young girls. Once they see the crime scene photos they may vote to execute him on the spot."

"Yeah, they'll want someone to pay for Jana Bell and Patton will be in front of them. But what if it is one of those cases? One of your cases. What if he's being set up? I didn't like the way his wife smiled when we took him out. What if she had something to do with it? What if he's innocent and we send him away?"

Strongly suspecting that she already knew and wouldn't like the answer, Bianca asked again, "What do you want?"

"He's willing to talk, that is, his lawyer is finally letting him talk. But not to me or McLarney or Erickson. His lawyer asked for you."

"Who's this lawyer?"

"Malcolm Henderson."

"He's one of the best. Why me?"

Beth shrugged. "Who knows?"

The conversation then turned to other cases and personal matters. When the two detectives were about to leave, "Just remember, Bianca, Patton likes them young. Dress accordingly."

Was that a joke or a warning? Probably the latter. Beth knew that Bianca was sensitive about her size and appearance.

All her life Bianca had been at war with her size, her shape. When all the other girls grew tall and shapely, Bianca had stopped growing, stopped developing. When she joined the BPD, she was used on hooker patrol as pedophile bait. To be taken seriously she developed a hard shell and a harder attitude, fighting for every decent assignment and for the respect commonly afforded her fellow officers. True, she had sometimes used her size and appearance when working a case, but always for reasons of her own. Maybe this time she should ….

No, she'd be damned if she'd give some teen raper jerk-off material. She decided to take Beth's comment as a warning and wear something professional.

Bianca met Malcolm Henderson and his client in the interview room of what had been the Baltimore City Jail and was now the Maryland Detention Center. Patton looked bad. His face bore several bruises in various stages of healing and he moved stiffly, as if his whole body ached. Even if he were innocent, Bianca did not feel sorry for him. She had seen what was on his computer.

"Prison life's rough for a kiddie killer, isn't it, Patton?"

"Please, Sergeant Jones, my client is in jail, not prison. And he of course maintains his innocence. While some of his actions may have been questionable and ill-advised they certainly were not criminal."

"Duly noted, Mr. Henderson. You wanted to talk. Why me?"

Malcolm Henderson sat back and studied the young detective before him. He had heard rumors about her, stories that he could not believe yet could not afford to ignore. Was this small woman really the Baltimore equivalent of Carl Kolchak? Was she truly the BPD's investigator of the weird? Henderson prided himself on being a rational man and so he did not think so. But he was trained to go where the evidence led. And after what Tony Patton had finally told him, the attorney had to take the chance that the rumors might be right.

"Because, Sergeant Jones, from all I've heard about you, you may be my client's only hope. Tell Sergeant Jones what you told me, Tony."

***

It had been a hell of Saturday afternoon, Tony Patton began. Golf and frustration. Not only was I off my game, but one of those scattered showers that Channel 45 weather gal had promised caught me at the tenth hole. I would've quit but my boss insisted we finish the game. So I was wet, tired and down fifty bucks.

When I got home I saw that the wife's car was gone. Then I remembered she was supposed to go out with a friend. I decided that it would be a good day to spend some time on my computer. After a hot shower and a change of clothes of course.

Then I walked into my living room and saw that Mitzi had been shopping again.

I don't know what is with that woman? Yard sales, flea markets, estate sales, antique shops. She can't resist any of them. And she buys something in all of them – books, lamps, statues, paintings, any old thing as long as it's old. She's convinced that one day she'll find a prize, a treasure that she can sell on eBay for a fortune.

Let me tell you, most of the shit she buys does get sold on eBay. I wind up selling it, usually at a loss. What's not sold winds up in the Goodwill donation bin, expect for the shit Mitzi hangs on the walls or sets around the house. "It makes the place look homey," she says. Homely is more like it.

So I looked over what Mitzi had piled on the sofa hoping that maybe this time she had brought home something useful. It was just the usual junk so I left it there for her to put away and went upstairs for a shower only to find more crap in the bedroom. There was old jewelry, yellowed postcards and what looked like half a bible messing up her dresser. On my bureau were three decks of playing cards, a toy truck without a rear tire and a kerosene lantern.

The truck was a waste, might as well throw the money she paid for it right into the trash. I didn't check but I was sure that none of those three decks of cards were complete. Which would be about right, my dumb bitch of a wife hasn't been playing with a full deck for years, not since she started all this buying shit.Now the kerosene lantern, that looked like it might actually be worth something. The only problem I could see with it with that was that its chimney was all clouded with film.

But at the time I had more important things to do than worry over what my wife had wasted money on. I was thinking about a shower, fresh clothes and the Internet.

But for some reason I was drawn back to the lamp. Whatever was clouding the chimney looked to be on the inside, and it seemed to be moving. It was some kind of mist, one that sort of swirled around inside the chimney. I got thinking that this was a cross between a railroad lantern and a lava lamp. Then for some reason I rubbed the lamp and the mist flowed out of it

Then a voice inside my head said, "Choose a pleasing shape."

I couldn't help it. When it said "a pleasing shape" all I could think about was this girl I'd seen around the neighborhood. Yeah, it was Jana Bell and I'd been thinking about her shape ever since last summer when I saw her in shorts and a tank top.

Then that voice said, "As you wish" and where the mist had been there was Jana, all blonde and fourteen, wearing the school girl outfit I'd been picturing her in.

I knew it wasn't her, couldn't be her, and that's what made what I did next sort of okay. I'm not saying it was right, but it wasn't her so it wasn't wrong either.

Then this … genie I guess it was, asked, "Does this form please you, Master?"

What the Hell, I'd thought it up, of course it did. I nodded and it said,

"I am here to please you, Master. To grant your every wish, your every desire. What is it you desire, Master?"

Okay, there was a lot I could have asked for – money, power, a new car, a bigger house, a better looking wife who was willing to go down on me. And maybe I was gonna wish for those things after. But right then, there was only one thing I wanted. I grabbed what was in front of me, threw her on the bed and did her hard.

Like I said, I knew this wasn't real. Maybe I was dreaming, maybe, I don't know. I did know it wasn't Jana, at least I thought it wasn't. She cried a little when I stuck it in, but that was part of the fantasy and it was a good one. Hell, it was a great one. Then just as I got off inside her I heard my wife shouting.

I looked up and saw Mitzi and her lezzie friend Hester standing in the doorway. My first thought was that maybe I should have first wished not to get caught. Then I thought that maybe it wasn't too late, that maybe I could wish those two back downstairs with a case of amnesia.

Then that genie started acting like the real Jana and that bitch I married was talking about me going to jail.

You can be sure that when she left me alone I went right to the lamp. Only there was no mist in its chimney and no matter how hard I rubbed it no genie came back.

That's when I started thinking I was in some serious trouble. I looked down at myself and saw blood on my pecker, Jana's blood or so it seemed. There was also some blood on the sheets. That's when I knew that I was well and truly screwed. Eh, no pun intended.

***

Not wanting to interrupt, Bianca had saved her questions until after Patton had finished his statement.

"So that's your defense, that you wet dreamed of genie?" Bianca shook her head. "And then what? Were you afraid that somehow this genie had conjured the real Jana Bell for you to rape so you wished for it to murder her?"

At Henderson's nod Patton answered. "No, like I told you, I only saw that genie once. After it ran out on me I never saw it again."

"So you say. At any time did you say anything like 'I wish that little bitch was dead?' and by bitch I mean Jana and not your wife."

"I didn't think it was really Jana. Why would I wish her dead? I didn't wish anyone dead. The only thing I wished was that the whole thing never happened. And I didn't get that wish, did I?"

"No, you didn't. Where did you get Jana's panties?"

"I didn't know they were there. I never saw them in my life."

"Just so we're clear on one thing. You mentioned wanting to use the computer, on planning to go online. Were two of the sites you were planning to visit …" Bianca made a show of looking at her notes, '… High School Cuties' and 'Hot Asian Teens?'"

Henderson stopped his client from answering. "Your department has Mr. Patton's computer. They know full well what sites he's been on. Unless things have changed, he's charged with murder, not some minor victimless sex offenses."

"Looking at and saving sexually explicit pictures of underaged girls is not a minor offense, counselor, and it's not victimless. It's called child pornography. But you're right, your client has not been charged with that, not yet anyway."

"About Mr. Patton's statement?"

"I'll look into it."

There was shock and maybe a little hope in Patton's voice. "You believe me?"

"Not yet, Patton, but it's possible. This is Baltimore. Stranger things have happened."

***

"So it was a genie?" asked Tammy Dolan. The criminalist had met with Bianca and Beth Steele in the back of Morgan's Books to discuss the case.

"Djinn," corrected Joe Russo from behind a stack of dusty books.

"Makes sense. Answers a lot of questions." Beth was behind a bottle of very fine wine that Joe had supplied from the store's cellar, a cellar that wasn't supposed to be there.

Tammy reached for the bottle and refilled her glass. "So what do you think? Did he wish Jana into the sack then wish her dead?"

"If he had possession of the gen..." Bianca looked toward the stack of books that hid her husband, "...djinn, none of this would be happening. The girl might still be dead but Patton would have wished himself off the hook. We think his wife set him up. Beth?"

Taking photos from a folder, the homicide detective showed them around. "This is Mitzi six months ago. This is her now."

The more recent pictures Beth passed around showed a much younger, much healthier looking Mitzi Patton. There was no grey in her hair, no lines on her face and it seemed that her breasts were slightly larger with less sag.

More photos. "This is her car. Again, from both six months ago and from last week. It's the same car."

"It looks newer," Tammy said.

"It's not newer, it's new. From what I was able to tell it's showroom fresh and probably always will be."

"Find a car you like and stick with it. Smart woman. No reason for anyone to question how she could afford a new car. Probably never needs gas either. If we're able to nail her for this that car's getting impounded and I'm buying it at the police auction."

"Only if you outbid me, Bianca." Beth handed the other two women financial documents. "The mortgage on the Patton home has now been paid. All credit card debts have been covered and there's a nice chunk of change left in the bank. Nothing too flashy, nothing suspicious, unless you're thinking wishes."

Bianca nodded. "Patton said his wife bought a lot of stuff from yard sales and the like. Guess she finally found the treasure she was looking for."

"And her first wish was probably to get rid of the pervert husband who treated her like dirt. Can't argue with her motive, just her methods."

Bianca nodded. "If a real person hadn't been involved and murdered, I'd agree, Tammy. Mitzi probably didn't expect her husband to imagine someone real, someone she knew. That might have pushed her to the edge."

"And when the plan fell through she went over that edge and wished the girl dead," added Beth. "But it's all theory for now. First we have to prove there is a djinn and then we have to ... how do you fight a genie?"

"You don't." Joe came around from his stack of books. "I've been researching this all day. I've read the Secret Writings of Solomon, Burton's original translation of The Arabian Nights and some Islamic texts that are as old as that creed itself. I've been on the phone with the DMA and a street vendor in Manhattan who keeps a djinn in his hot dog cart."

Joe sat down next to his wife and took a sip from her glass. "Say one thing for Morgan, he had great tastes in books and wines." Joe was quiet for a moment as he thought about the man from whom he had inherited the book shop, a man who had given his life in the fight against Evil.

"The Djinn are creatures of immense power, they can warp reality itself. Unlike the other creatures we've faced – vampires, werewolves, mythos beasts – there's nothing we can exploit. Even the Devil had limitations. The Djinn are magic itself but it's magic that can only be exercised at a mortal's whim. That's their punishment for a sin of Pride that stopped just short of rebellion against Heaven. If she has a djinn's vessel, there's nothing to stop Mitzi Patton from wishing for us to leave her alone, forget the investigation, or just plain drop dead."

"I thought genies couldn't kill."

"Jana Bell probably thought so too, Tammy," Joe replied, maybe a bit too harshly. "The only way to stop this woman is to get the vessel without letting her know you're looking for it."

"Or take her out."

All of them knew what Beth meant. All of them had thought about it. It was Tammy who raised the obvious objections.

"There's no proof there really is a genie. Or that Mitzi Patton has one. And like Joe said, we're not going against a monster like a witch or a demon. Mitzi is human. What if we're wrong? She'll be dead, the genie'll still be loose and we'll be like the monsters we hunt."

"So we go in, with or without a warrant, and grab every lamp in the place."

Joe spoke up. "I said a vessel, Beth, it doesn't have to be a lamp. It could be anything that holds something – a cup, a bottle, a box. If I had control of a djinn I'd keep it in my cell phone. At least I wouldn't have any more dropped calls."

"What about that DNA trick you and Bianca did with that witch?" Beth suggested. "Could we do that?"

"The Djinn are creatures of fire, not earth like us. I suspect that the residue found on Jana's body and the Pattons' bedsheet is a close as to DNA as we're likely to come. Anything on that, Tammy?"

When the Criminalist shook her head Bianca told her, "Bottle what's left." When the other three looked at her she explained, "A djinn's essence in a bottle. It's not much of an advantage but it's all we've got. The first thing is to get into the house when Mitzi's not home and maybe find out if there is a djinn. Maybe our bottled genie juice will help. If there is …"

Bianca closed her eyes and thought for a moment. "Joe, are you absolutely sure that there's no way of fighting this creature?"

"None that I can find."

With her eyes still closed Bianca sighed and said, "A killer with a mystical weapon of destruction. Screw it. Joe, if anything happens to Beth or me, send word to Tavon. Tell him to take Mitzi Patton into custody and throw her naked into a cell. Then burn down her house and bury anything that's left as deep as possible."

And pray that's enough, Bianca added silently.

Later that night, as they were getting ready for bed, Joe asked Bianca, "You're thinking of the djinn, aren't you?"

Bianca's look told him he was right.

"A djinn would be a powerful weapon, if it was used right. But the wrong word, the wrong phrasing could be disastrous." Joe stopped, knowing that he didn't have to explain, that his wife would know what he meant.

She did, but she wasn't thinking of weapons. Her wishing was more personal – height, curves, breasts. A better life away from Baltimore, maybe a family. No more monsters, no more screaming houses, no more danger to her and Joe.

"If you had the lamp, what would be your wish?"

Looking at the woman he loved, Joe said, "Everything I want is right in front of me."

Bianca got into bed smiling. Eventually they contentedly fell asleep in each other's arm.

***

The warrant on the Patton home was obtained on the basis that there might be digital media – thumb drives, SD cards, CDs and DVDs – containing sexually explicit images of young girls still in the house. Given the small size of the objects for which they were supposedly searching, this gave Beth and Bianca license to look anywhere in the house.

The warrant was served on a Saturday morning not five minutes after Mitzi Patton left for her weekly scavenger hunt at yard sales, flea markets and the like.

Each woman had a bottle containing a small amount of the essence believed to be from the djinn. "When we get inside," Beth said, "You go upstairs and I'll take the first floor. Call out if you find anything."

Bianca agreed. The detectives entered then found themselves outside the front door with no idea how they got there.

"Bianca, what just happened?"

"I think I know. Wait here." Again, Bianca entered. When she did not reappear Beth was about to go in when Bianca came around from the back.

"Outside the kitchen door this time." Bianca went in a third time, but not before uncapping her bottle of genie juice.

"I wish you'd stop that," she shouted as soon as she was inside.

If I could. The voice was inside her head. *It is my master's wish that I protect this house and all its contents.*

"I have no designs on this house," Bianca said quickly, then, surrendering to the situation, added, "or any of its contents."

Finding herself still inside, the detective asked, "You are a djinn?"

No answer.

"Was Tony Patton your master?"

It was wished that he believe himself so.

"So your master is Mitzi Patton?"

No answer.

"Did you kill Jana Bell?"

No answer, then,

I must obey my master's wishes.

"What of your own wishes."

My kind may not wish.

"If you could, for what would you wish?"

At first Bianca thought that there was no answer, then in a tiny corner of her mind came a faint whisper.

Freedom.

"Where is your vessel?"

The voice grew louder. *It is my master's wish that I protect this house – and all its contents.*

Bianca found herself outside the house, staring at a panting Beth Steele.

"What happened to you?"

"I … tried to follow you in. The first time … back door. The … second time … across the street. The last time … four blocks away. Just … ran … back. How … how'd you do?"

"I think I got what we need." Bianca stepped back and looked at the house. What was it Joe had said, that a vessel is "anything that holds something?" A house can hold a lot of things, all its contents in fact.

"I have an idea. And if it doesn't work, we burn the house down."

If you destroy its vessel, do you destroy the genie, Bianca wondered. It would be a sort of freedom, she decided.

***

"Thank you for seeing us, Mrs. Patton."

Bianca and Beth were in the Pattons' living room. It was a few days after Bianca's conversation with the djinn. With Beth taking the lead Bianca sat quietly, hoping that Mitzi had not been warned.

"You said there was news about my husband's case? Good or bad?"

Knowing, or rather suspecting what they did, both detectives wondered what Mitzi would consider "bad news." Beth avoided the question.

"We've heard from Mr. Patton's attorney. He says that he has evidence that might clear your husband of the murder."

"But I saw him … with Jana. He was on top of her."

"We think that was someone your husband had made up to look like Jana," Beth explained. "It's possible that he was obsessed with her. At least, that will be the State's case against whatever the defense comes up with. And that's why we're here. We're looking for things that might strengthen the case. We seized your husband's digital camera but there were no files on it. Could he have taken photos of Jana?"

"He might have."

"Do you know of anywhere in the house he may have hidden the flash drives or SD cards the photos might be on?"

"I don't know, but I'll look around. If I find anything I'll let you know."

And if you don't, Bianca thought, you'll wish some up. Then she spoke for the first time.

"Let us know if you don't find anything as well."

Slightly confused, Mitzi looked at Beth who explained.

"It's negative evidence, Mrs. Patton. It would help the defense but we're still obliged to report it."

"And it's possible that your husband didn't kill the girl."

Mitzi turned to Bianca. "How can you say that? I mean, I know he's my husband but the evidence, what I saw ..."

"Just because we make an arrest that doesn't mean we stop investigating. There's always the chance that we missed something. We don't want to send an innocent man to jail. We want the right people to pay."

"We all wish that," Beth added. "Don't you, Mrs. Patton?"

"Of course I do."

It was not until the mist began forming in her living room that Mitzi Patton realized what she had said.

"No, I didn't mean, I mean ..."

A voice came from the mist. "A wish has been made. That wish shall be granted."

The mist grew solid, becoming a larger, more grotesque version of Tony Patton. Neither detective moved to stop it as it reached out for Mitzi.

With the woman in its grasp, it turned to Bianca and Beth.

"You must go now."

The two detectives found themselves on the sidewalk outside the house, listening to faint sounds of screaming.

Beth was ready to run back inside. "What's he doing to her?"

Bianca restrained her partner. "Administering justice," she said coldly. "No doubt by the most ancient of codes. An eye for an eye, etc."

"Doesn't that bother you?"

It should but it doesn't, Bianca thought, wondering just how much of her humanity her job had cost her. To Beth she replied,

"I saw the photos of what was done, what that woman had done to Jana Bell. You saw the girl's body. Think about that and tell me how much it bothers you."

Beth didn't reply but looking at the house she felt a little of her own humanity slipping away.

"How long do we wait?"

"Until the screaming stops."

Twenty minutes later they went in.

The nude body of Mitzi lay on the floor. Horribly abused, she had been sexually assaulted in every way possible before her throat was slit. Above her stood a bronzed-skinned young man who appeared to be in his late twenties.

"I have assumed the shape most pleasing to me," he said, "that shape which was my own at the time of the Great Sin and Condemnation."

"It's over now," Bianca said, wondering if the djinn would now reveal its vessel and if she dared become it master.

"Not yet. It was my late master's wish that the 'right people' pay the price of justice. Slave I might be, but I am still a person."

"You were a weapon," Bianca argued, "no more at fault than a gun or knife."

"A weapon does not feel guilt over its actions. A weapon does not feel the shame of the many evil things it was forced to do. A weapon does not feel the degradation of centuries of slavery. I choose not to be a weapon. I choose to be a slave no longer. To fulfill my master's final wish, I choose to be mortal so that I may pay the price of justice."

Then in a whispered voice the djinn added, "I wish to be free."

He raised a bloody knife.

"Call in it, Beth," Bianca said calmly. "Signal 13. Officers on scene with an armed murder suspect."

The djinn slowly advanced, giving the detectives all the time they needed. As Beth worked the radio, Bianca drew her service pistol, took careful aim and with two shots granted him his wish.

With Beth in the background calling in "Shots fired, suspect down" Bianca rushed to the fallen djinn. Not yet dead, he was clearly dying.

His voice was whispered, his breath labored. "The things I was forced to do, I pray that they will not be counted against me come the Judgment."

Bianca hoped so as well. His wish had been for freedom. He should not be denied the chance. But there was nothing she could do. Unless … but do I dare, she wondered.

To save souls from Hell, Bianca had challenged demons. She had defied angels. She had risked damnation and refused Heaven. To save one more soul she would dare anything.

"What was your name," she asked the dying man, "your true name?"

"Once, I was known as Farhoud."

Bianca spoke quickly, knowing she was racing death as well as approaching sirens.

"Farhoud, for all the many sins of your long life, no matter how or why you committed them, are you truly sorry and repentant?"

"Yes," answered a fading voice.

"Then you are forgiven them."

As Bianca finished speaking cars with screaming sirens pulled up outside. She felt the life leave Farhoud's body and prayed that she had not been too late. She didn't think so. She remembered once reading that it was the confession and not the priest that granted absolution.

And just before the two detectives were swept up in the administrative chaos that comes with a police-involved shooting Bianca prayed that it was true. Prayed that the genie's first wish had been granted.

GOD AFTER GOD

by

John L. French and C.J. Henderson

"One of the chief pretenders to the throne of God is radio itself, which has acquired a sort of omniscience. I live in a strictly rural community, and people here ... when they say "the Radio," they don't mean a cabinet, an electronic phenomenon, or a man in a studio, they refer to a pervading and godlike presence which has come into their lives and homes." E.G. White

"I guess television just has more power than any of us know." Ronald Reagan

As a child, Lora Dean had not been afraid of the dark. Even after being told stories of "the bogey man," and other bits of shared nonsense used to frighten the young, she had remained comfortable even when in total darkness. Her parents had always been pleased to announce to anyone who would listen that Lora's room had never held a night light. As an adult, however, Lora had not only learned to fear the darkness …

She had learned terror at even the approach of shadows.

The fear first manifested itself when her boss, Marvin Richards, host of the sometimes top-rated television show Challenge of the Unknown, got his hands on a diary written by someone called "Mad Berkley." It was rumored that in London some thirty years ago this book had caused the death, the physical dissolution in fact, of three men who had dared to perform one of the damned rites found within it pages.

Despite this rumor, or maybe because of it, Richards had it read live on the air and predictably, darkness fell over the Earth. Bugg Shash, the Shambler, He Who Comes in Darkness, the Stygian Hunger, had been summoned. And for a moment, that ravenous demon god which had preyed on humanity for eons thought it had struck the mother lode. The horror possessed the ability to atomize the flesh and soul of any it found within the dark. For thousands of years that had meant one or two victims at a time – five, tops.

But, this time it had been summoned to a banquet table set with not only the tens of thousands there in the arena from which the episode was being broadcast, but possibly all life on the planet. With millions upon millions of sets turned on all over the world, the thing had been presented with a once-in-a-millennia opportunity to fly through the ebony of the void and consume billions.

But the world got lucky. Bugg Shash was a god of the night, a shadow thing that traveled in darkness. Having been summoned through the magic of television, the beast-thing manifested not in one particular locale but across the face of the Earth, a place – as you know – always half steeped in night, and half in day. The Shambler was torn apart at the sub-atomic level. Not a single soul was lost. But television history was made.

Challenge of the Unknown had done it again. Not only had the live event produced the show's highest ratings and market share to date, but it also rapidly became the most heavily downloaded (legally or otherwise) television event in the chronicles of the medium. Special DVD and 3D Blu Ray discs were released, with enhanced effects, a musical score composed by the fastest working (if not the best) of Hollywood's composers, and a commentary track featuring Richards, Stephen Hawking and a trio of clairvoyants who claimed to be channeling Aleister Crowley, Pope John the XXIII and Soupy Sales (the presence of whom on the extra made it a shoe-in for a major mention at Ain't It Cool News as well as an MTV Award).

None of this financial success helped Lora Dean, however. While certain she was not the only one to understand the import of what they had accomplished, she was the only one of whom she was aware.

"Did we really kill ... a god ... just for higher ratings," she had asked Richards afterwards. His reply was the first thing that frightened her.

"Sure looks that way, don't it," he had answered glibly, still dreaming of the riches to come. As he speculated within his head as to the revenues they might expect, he had added;

"Ain't it cool?"

The second thing to frighten her was the speculation that perhaps the Devourer was not dead, but that it was merely lurking somewhere in the darkness, waiting to take its revenge.

For the longest time afterward, Lora could not bear the dark. Gradually, as time passed and there were no reports of people being turned into pools of slime by an angry Shambler (or by anything else which could conceivably be translated to indicate the return of Bugg-Shash), her fears faded to where a night light in her bedroom and one in her hall were sufficient for her peace of mind. Her parents were disappointed, but at least she could sleep.

It was after their second trip to the zombie infested town of Wixom that Lora began to notice shadows once more. Shadows that mysteriously lengthened or shrank. Shadows seemingly not cast by anything tangible – shadows that moved for no reason. Shadows which restored to Lora the fear she had thought safely passed.

"It's back."

"What's back," asked Marvin Richards. Seated behind his desk, reviewing proposed segments for the next season's shows, he spoke without looking, "Disco? The Economy? Bridget Loves Bernie?"

"It. The god you killed."

"Could you be more specific? There are so …"

Finally looking up, Richards saw fear shining within Lora's eyes. Not just "fear," but "The Fear," the fear she had fallen into after the Shambler episode.

Oh, thought the anchorman, suddenly feeling not quite so glib, that's what's back.

Seeing his assistant in such a state worried Richards. Lora was not one to panic – not anymore. She had come to Challenge with the healthy fear of any person intelligent enough to realize that striking matches could ignite a conflagration (something of a rare attribute in someone working in television and only one of the reasons he valued her so) and he had thought he was going to lose her after the leprechaun segment. But she had toughened up and stood with him through an array of other dangerous, life-threatening assignments.

She had conquered The Fear and stayed around for more. Not foolish enough to ignore what her renewed fear meant, he asked;

"What makes you think so?"

"Haven't you seen the shadows?" Lora pointed towards the door which she had left open. From the way it stood ajar light from the hall cast its shadow on the office floor, a shadow that when studied closely appeared to extend too far for the size of the door. Taking note of this caused Richards to study the other shadows in his office. Were they the right size? Could some of them be moving? Was one of them actually extending an angry middle digit in his direction?

"I see what you mean."

Without another word Richards stood, then turned on every light in the office. Once all trace of shadow had been purged from the room he returned to his desk. Reaching into a drawer he pulled out a file which he passed to Lora.

"I've been saving this."

"Baltimore," she said, reading the folder's label. "City of the Weird."

"Interesting place," offered Richards as Lora leafed through the file's contents. "Lots of strange activity in that city, from before Poe up to the present day. Reports of extra dimensional creatures, werewolves, vampires, government created freaks and even infernal visitations. And in the center of it all …"

The producer paused for effect as Lora came to a particular photograph. It was a standard ID head and torso shot of a not very special looking young woman. Lora could tell that, despite her slender, somewhat undeveloped frame, the woman was not as young as most people probably thought at first glance.

"That, my dear, is the Bianca Jones. The Crabtown equivalent of New York's Twilight Squad."

"Crabtown...?"

"They like crabs in Baltimore, eat 'em by the bucketful. Restaurants give the customers hammers. It's a great custom."

"Un-huh ... and this woman ... when she's not smashing crabs open …"

"Is the Baltimore PD's supernatural cop. Rumor has it she has personally kicked the ass of every monster from Delaware to Virginia. I'm thinking maybe it's time to do some stories on Baltimore's weird past and present."

"If she's the Dirty Harriet of the Weird, then why haven't we done a story on her already?"

Lora stared at her boss, giving him a look she only used when she needed him to know it was no time for face-saving. Richards began to answer her twice, sputtering as his charm slammed up against his teeth, refusing to be uttered lest his assistant turn up the intensity of her gaze and fry him on the spot. Finally able to break eye contact, Richards muttered;

"Ms. Jones, ahhhh …"

"Yes...?"

"Ummmmm ... Detective Jones then, Sergeant Jones now …"

"Go on...,"

"Hiiiihh ... oh, what the hell, she said she would kick my ass and worse if I ever set foot in her jurisdiction again."

"Again?"

"I really do talk too much around you."

Smiling, knowing that such a statement from Richards was practically a declaration of love, Lora merely tilted her head. Understanding that he had just been ordered to let the other shoe drop, the anchorman said;

"Before you joined our little family here, she had just started making a name for herself in our circles ..."

"And, you went down to do a story on her ..."

"Right ..."

"And you tried to slut her up for the cameras ..."

"Hey, it wasn't that bad." Seeing no trace of belief in his assistant's eyes, Richards admitted;

"All I said was that Victoria's Secret had nothing to do with anti-gravity, just paradigm-altering wiring ..."

"And she didn't deck you?"

"Several of her fellow officers intervened on my behalf."

"But now," whispered a voice within the young woman's mind as she stared at the producer unblinking, half-looking at the photograph in her hand at the same time, "you get a case of the willies and he's ready to take his chances going across the Maryland state line."

"Okay," said Lora, shoving aside the thought of moving shadows and living darkness, "let's go to Baltimore."

"You're not afraid?"

"I'm afraid," she responded, "that the show must go on."

"Yeah," answered Richards, not joking at all, "I'm always afraid of that, too."

***

"No."

Not many officers of the Baltimore Police Department would refuse a direct order from its Commissioner. Sergeant Bianca Jones was one of them.

"I don't recall giving you a choice, Sergeant Jones."

Not good, thought the officer. Had he called me "Bianca" there'd be some room for discussion. Still, it's not like I've ever willingly given up a fight.

"Commissioner, allowing Challenge of the Unknown to film in Baltimore is asking for trouble. My kind of trouble. Richards and his crew are a danger not only to themselves and those around them but to the nation – the whole world."

"Sergeant ..."

"Hundreds of thousands dead after one episode. Hundreds of thousands! Richards is a maniac – he's let loose werewolves and vampires ... we're still getting calls from people who swear their homes are infested with cockroach fairies ..."

"Yes," admitted the commissioner, "and he's been investigated each time and found not to be legally responsible. None of the indictments were sustained and most of the civil suits dismissed."

"Not legally responsible." Bianca uttered the phrase as if it were a curse. "What about morally responsible?"

"Oh, for God's sake, he's in show business." Sighing heavily, the commissioner held back the first comment that came to his mind, then said;

"Bianca, the mayor wants this. She sees Challenge as a way to boost the city, get us some good press, get a new breed of tourists flowing ... out-of-towners bring in money and jobs."

"And money and jobs equals votes?"

The commissioner shrugged. "Were you expecting politicians to be better than TV people?" When the sergeant made no reply, her superior gave her the news he had been holding back.

"Richards asked for you specifically."

"I'm not going on television."

"No one's asking you to. Richards, or rather his assistant said they want you there as a technical adviser in case, and I quote, 'things go wrong.'"

"That only tells me one thing, Commissioner."

"That for once Richards is being morally responsible?"

"No, that he's planning something that will probably go wrong."

"And, if it does, I expect you to handle it in your usual efficient manner – and to arrest all those responsible."

Bianca smiled. Apparently there had been room for discussion after all.

***

Richards's production company rented a recently closed Catholic school as their Baltimore headquarters. Empty classrooms were used as offices, dressing rooms, prop storage and the such. As a way to reduce costs as well as keep the staff centralized, the third floor was converted into dorms for the production staff. The school's spacious auditorium, the main asset which had attracted Richards in the first place, was converted into a studio.

"I'm sorry, Miss, you can't come in."

How do they find out so quickly, the guard at the school's front door wondered. Wherever we go, no matter how little we talk about it, there's always someone who hears about the show and wants to break into to TV.

Manny Fielding had been with Challenge since the beginning. He wondered for a moment what the girl before him would offer to be allowed entrance. Having two teenagers of his own, he pitied the inevitable fresh faces who would compromise themselves in any way suggested to break into the business.

"Didn't you hear, honey," he said with a smile, feeling as sorry for the girl before him as he had any of them, "school's closed for good. Go home and spread the word to all your FaceFriends."

"I really think you should let me in," the young looking woman said as she unzipped her jacket, pulling back its left side to reveal a very large pistol.

For a moment Manny froze, suddenly convinced all the stories that he had about Baltimore were true. Then he noticed that the woman was not reaching for her gun, but rather the police badge clipped next to it.

"Sergeant Bianca Jones to see ... Mr. Richards."

Wordlessly Manny pointed toward the auditorium.

"Thanks ... honey," Bianca said as she left the guard and went looking for Richards. She found him discussing the studio arrangements with his assistant. As Bianca drew closer, Richards brought their discussion to a halt, turning to greet the officer.

"Ms. Jones, Detective Jones, Sergeant Jones ... am I being polite enough for you this time?"

Recognizing the look in the detective's eyes, knowing what the officer would most likely prefer to do to her boss, Lora stepped into the awkward situation. Extending her hand, she said in a voice calculated to reveal nothing of what she knew about their situation;

"Sergeant Jones, so nice to meet you. I'm Lora Dean, Marv's executive assistant. So nice of you to come."

"I go where I'm ordered, Ms. Dean. Now if there's a place for us to talk?"

Five minutes time found the trio in the conference room within what had formerly been the Principal's suite. Thinking that it would probably be best to clear the air between them up front, Richards asked in his happiest tone;

"So, still want to kick my ass, Sergeant?"

"Why yes, I do," Bianca replied honestly, her smile so wide it hurt the corners of her mouth. "More than you can imagine."

"See," said the anchorman in a pleasant tone to Lora, "just like I told you. As charming as she is tall." When the detective bristled, Richards held up a hand, saying;

"All right. I just wanted to get all the crap out in the open so no one trips over it. And, for the record, I know, and can understand, why you feel about me the way you do."

"You think so, eh," asked Bianca, congratulating herself on being able to answer the producer without grinding her teeth.

"Sure. I've heard all the criticisms, suffered through the arrests and court hearings. Like all the others looking for a place to dump their leftover blame, you think I'm the Nazi-psycho-killer-madman responsible for nine tenths of the macabre deaths in this world."

"What a keen grasp of the obvious you have," responded Bianca in a flat tone. "No wonder you're so successful."

"You're right about that. I am successful. But at what? Don't volunteer an answer, I'll tell you. I am the best there is at providing news and entertainment of a particular bend. I have a great knack for shining a light on the things that go bump in the night. Now, we all know a good ninety percent of what ends up on the show is bullshit ... haunted houses with no spirits, mummies that never walked, low rent witches and tarot dealers ..."

"It's the other ten percent I'm interested in."

"So's our audience. That's why they watch. For that wonderful, thank-you-Jesus every-so-often when something real happens. And yeah, when it does, you'd better believe I don't shy away from it. Like any good newsman I report it. But, those times when people die, it's not because of anything I did. Some die because they were just in the wrong place. Most of them, though, died because they were greedy or lazy or just wanted an easy way out."

"And you feel no responsibility at all for their deaths?"

Richards paused for a moment, wondering if he would be believed if he admitted to just how many times he had asked himself that question. Knowing such would do him no good, he went instead with the line he had rehearsed for the moment he knew would come when the detective confronted him.

"What I feel, Sergeant Jones, is none of your business. Just as how you feel about your role in the fires and riots that ravaged your city not so long ago is none of my business."

Noting the slight surprise that came over Bianca's face, Richards went on. "Yes, I know the real story and not the one given out to the 'legitimate' media. God, they're so naive. How often do you ask yourself what, or rather, who caused the devil to attack Baltimore so viciously?"

Bianca admitted to herself that Richards had indeed turned the tables quite neatly on her as she again counted the cost of her battle with the master of Hell. Thousands slaughtered, more wounded, her partner nearly killed, forced into retirement – and worse, the man who had been the Police Commissioner hounded from office and narrowly escaping a prison sentence merely for giving the orders that saved the city.

Could she have done anything different, she asked herself again. If she had known the cost, would she have acted as she did? She had yet to answer those questions or any of the others that screamed within her head so often. Ignoring them, fixing the anchorman with the look which had shaken murderers and rapists, she admitted;

"Every damn night."

"And yet you keep on doing your job," said Richards softly. "As do I. And now, speaking of doing our jobs, what's your understanding of your current assignment, Ms. Jones?"

Shocked to find herself suddenly giving the producer the benefit of at least half a doubt, Bianca replied;

"I'm to assist you in the stories you plan to do about Baltimore's supernatural past and present, answering all your questions as best I can and cautioning you about certain cases that are too sensitive for discussion or that have not yet been safely resolved."

"Such as the disappearing house in Southwest Baltimore?" Not surprised to hear that the Challenge crews had learned about that, Bianca simply smiled.

"It's reappeared again."

"And if we were to try to go into that house?"

"Oh, I'd let you." Enjoying the look on Richards' face at her ambiguity, Bianca continued. "As I said, my job is to caution you against doing anything stupid, not to prevent you from doing it."

"Sort of like the warnings on the DVD sets of our TV show."

Bianca turned to Lora, smiling to show she appreciated the woman's quick wit, as well as her honesty. Begrudgingly beginning to feel that working with the Challenge team might not be the worst assignment she had ever been handed, she said;

"My job is also to provide security. Starting later today, members of a special unit of the BPD's Quick Response Team will be brought in. These officers have been trained to handle any ... unusual ... incidents that might arise. I should add that these officers have also been trained to recognize when someone is trying to summon a demon, a spirit or anything similar."

"I sense a hidden meaning in your tone, Ms. Jones."

"Just saying that their trained response would be to shoot to kill to prevent such a summoning." Smiling once more, beginning to enjoy the ache from the uncustomary use of the muscles necessary to do so, she added;

"Do we understand each other?"

"More than you know, Sergeant."

Staring into a corner where she had been watching one shadow in particular grow and shrink, Lora joined the conversation once more, asking;

"Marv, shouldn't we tell the sergeant about ... shall we say, what happens these days when the lights go out?"

As Richards nodded in agreement, Lora told Bianca of her newly returned fear of shadows and the actual reason Challenge of the Unknown had come to Baltimore.

* * *

"So," Richards asked after all had been revealed, "what would you suggest, Sergeant?"

"The obvious. Bright lights dispel shadows. Keep rooms well-lit and powerful flashlights at hand at all times."

"And at night?"

"What can I tell you, Ms. Dean? Whether what's going on is a return of Bugg-Shash, or something else filtering through from its dimension, I'd say you can at least take it as a good sign that whatever it is hasn't attacked yet."

"And, is there anything you can do?"

"I'm sure there probably is, Mr. Richards," answered Bianca, standing up out of her chair. Heading for the door, she added, "And if I think of what that might be, you'll be the first person I tell."

The detective found that the idea that Richards might not simply be money-hungry scum had invaded her mind, souring all the splendid insults she had been dreaming up since she had first been told she would have to work with him. In a world filled with horrors from beyond – horrors in which most refused to believe – Challenge did serve a useful purpose. Every person it convinced vampires were real, for instance, was one less easy target.

Heading back to her office, Bianca put aside most of her resentment and began to mentally construct possible defenses. She planned to watch the Bugg Shash DVD and again study the news reports about the show's aftermath. Maybe she'd play the DVD and study the shadows in her office.

One perk of the sergeant's Special Operation assignment was a HQ parking space. The garage had been built at the same time as Police Headquarters and was the only part of the building that had not been updated at least twice. Cold in the winter, steaming in the summer, it was perpetually dark with only half its lights working at any one time. Old as it was, Bianca liked it. It was one of the few things about the BPD that had not changed since she had been a rookie. The temperature swings were not that bothersome. And usually, the darkness did not bother her.

Usually.

The detective has just left her car when she noticed the shadows. The ones that were not quite right. The size of them, possibly their angle. Using her vehicle's spot light, Bianca lit one up. It disappeared, then returned when the light was extinguished. It was, however, a slightly different shape.

Okay, thought the sergeant, that didn't take long.

***

Bianca had learned early on in dealing with monsters that it generally was a good idea to take the battle to them. Not used to resistance, they usually made a mistake which would end up giving her an edge. She chose a mostly empty room, partly lit so as to throw shadows against one wall, hurriedly rigged with arc lights for when something happened. The audio file ripped from the Shambler DVD set to play on her laptop, Bianca was ready to see what would happen if the shadows were confronted within a controlled environment.

Crossing her fingers, the sergeant hit "play" on her computer. The chanting started. At first, nothing happened. The audio file looped and played again as Bianca watched the darkness on the far wall. With the fifth repetition it moved. On the sixth it seemed to get thicker.

Sensing time might be running out, Bianca hit the jury-rigged switch next to her. The ebony swirl just beginning to congeal into a humanoid shape froze as lights brighter than day pinned it into a corner.

"Can you hear me? Understand me?" At first the man-like shadow nodded, then sound filtered through the air.

I/we do/can hear you ... understand

Not concerning herself with how such a being could speak without vocal cords, Bianca asked;

"What do you want?"

Justice

Bianca nodded, her curiosity aroused.

"For whom, against whom?"

For me/us, against the God Killer ... soon ... when strong enough ... I/we will drag the God Killer to his fate

"That's not justice. It's vengeance," Bianca replied, even while thinking that it was nothing less than she would do – nothing less than she had done.

The same to me/us ... The God Killer will, must pay

"It's not the same to me."

No matter ... I/we are everywhere ... When I/we are strong enough ...

"No," Bianca said emphatically, "you will not."

You will not/cannot stop me/us

Almost casually, Bianca moved one of the lights until it touched the shadow form. The man shape drew back in obvious pain.

"Take it from one who knows, open portals go both ways. If he whom you call God Killer is taken, if any of his followers are attacked, I will find a way through and I will bring a light far greater than this one. Light killed your god. What will it do to your world?"

You would do this horrible thing ... To protect one man you would destroy a world

Would I? Bianca asked herself.

Merely to save Richards, she knew she would not. But, she reasoned, if the shadows could take the producer, then they could take anyone – or everyone.

"And when they came for me," the detective whispered. Her face going grim, she said aloud;

"Yes, I would."

Then if there is to be no justice for me/us/our god ...

The shadow-thing did not have to complete its threat. Bianca knew what it was implying – war. A conflict waged between shadow and light with vengeful creatures striking from the dark daring the light to strike back.

Feeling time evaporate all about her, the sergeant asked;

"You spoke of justice. What is that to your kind?"

Payment for what was, redressing what has been done, restoring the Balance

Nodding in understanding, Bianca made the only offer she could.

"Vengeance harms all. It cannot be allowed. But, if it's actually justice you want ... can you enter this world in, ummmm, a solid form?"

It is/will be difficult ... painful ... but can be done

"Then I have an idea."

***

"A trial?"

Standing behind what had once been a principal's desk, Marvin Richards wore a face perfectly designed to transmit incredulity. Waving one arm at his phone, he told it;

"We've been through this – I've been through this. I can't tell you how many indictments our legal team have had quashed ..."

"I can."

The voice coming from the newly installed speaker phone was that of Maxie Gerber, network liaison to Challenge of the Unknown.

"Eighty-seven as of last Tuesday. It's like every politician in any city with an upcoming election wants a piece of you, Marv. Not to mention your legal problems overseas. What is it now, eight countries you can't visit without chancing arrest? A public trial might be the just the thing to put this all behind us. Besides, think of the ratings."

As Gerber continued, Richards and Lora pictured the man sitting behind his desk, his hand in the air as if displaying a huge banner.

"Picture it, Marv. 'A Challenge of the Unknown Special. Marvin Richards versus the Creatures of Darkness. Tune in as he fights for his life against the horrors of the Shadow Realm.' We make it pay-per-view, we rake in a fortune."

"No pay-per-view."

"There's a depressing voice," responded the network man in a voice laced with sorrow. "And you are?"

"Sergeant Bianca Jones, Mr. Gerber."

"Call me Maxie, sweetheart. You're the one who set this up, aren't you. Great idea, honey. Say, if you ever tire of police work give me a call. We can build a great reality series around you. You'd be hotter than what's his name in Chicago."

"Thanks for the offer, Mr. Gerber," answered Bianca, "but if I ever want to sell my soul, the actual devil's got first refusal. So I won't be needing any of his demons in training."

"Cute. But why no pay-per-view?"

"The verdict is to be decided by those watching – telephone, text, Internet. If Mr. Richards is to have a chance he'll need the largest possible audience."

"Why?" asked Lora in honest confusion. "Yes, there are lots of people out there who don't like him." When the anchorman gave his assistant a hurt look, she rolled her eyes at him, then said to Bianca;

"There are people in this room that aren't always crazy about him. But there are millions that love him and the show. Besides, who would vote in favor of some alien monsters?"

"When I proposed that Mr. Richards be publicly tried for killing their god," explained the sergeant loud enough for Maxie to hear as well, "the Shadow Realm's representative readily agreed. Apparently that's how they settle things among themselves. As it was explained to me, while they each have an individual consciousness, they're also linked into a group mind. The disputing parties each argue their case and the overall consensus decides the outcome."

"A society with no need for lawyers. It's a beautiful thing. No offense, Maxie."

"Who could take offense at you, boychik," responded Gerber, rapidly adding, "But so what, this group brain thing? We're trying this here, not in the shadows, right?"

"Not exactly," explained Bianca. "To ensure their cooperation, it had to be agreed that the inhabitants of both worlds get to decide. We not only have to convince the people of this world Richards's not responsible for anything, but those of the other world as well."

Silence prevailed as the others realized the full impact of the detective's statement. Richards sank back in his chair, Lora reaching out and taking his hand. Finally, the producer asked;

"So, just for the sake of argument, what happens if I don't agree?"

"The shadows call you 'God Killer,' Mr. Richards. Sooner or later they'll come looking for their pound of flesh." Bianca glanced in Lora's direction, added;

"After they get one from you, they might cast about for one from someone else. Maybe more than one. What do we know about them? They might go after mankind."

"I'd ask what kind of creatures would blame a whole race for the actions of a few," came Gerber's voice from the speaker, "but my people have been asking that question for two thousand years. So tell me, sweetheart, what's your take on a bottom line here?"

"Worst case," answered Bianca, "the shadows take Mr. Richards ... maybe a few others. We retaliate. They escalate. Before you know it, we've got the War of the Worlds on our hands."

"She means for real this time, Maxie."

"I understand, Marv."

"No Orson Welles tap dance."

"I get it, I get it."

"Yeah," answered Richards, standing as he did so. "So do I." A thin trace of a smile crossing his face, he added;

"Well, what the hell? I certainly didn't mean for this nightmare to go to series, but if wishes and buts were candy and nuts, we'd all have a merry Christmas." Slapping his hands together, the anchorman announced;

"Well, these sci fi bozos want a show trial, let's give them a show trial – the biggest, grandest, most lavish embarrassment the legal system has ever seen."

"That's the spirit," came Gerber's voice over the speaker. "It'll be bigger than Simpson, bigger than Jackson, bigger than Scopes ..."

"Hell," declared Richards, "we do this thing right, this'll be the most talked about trial since the one Pilate held."

"Ohhh," sighed Gerber, "think of the ratings."

"But, Marv, I mean ... what if you lose?"

"Me? Lose? Oh Lora, my sweet child, oh ye of little faith." Understanding bravado more than most, Bianca asked;

"I've got as little faith in you as anyone, Richards. So, what is the answer? What if you lose?"

"Well, I never wanted to retire, anyway. So, if I have to go, if I get to die saving the world, saving two worlds – think of it, detective, I'll be remembered forever."

"Quite possible," admitted the sergeant.

"You bet it is. But, if I win, think of the ratings, think of the fame."

"Yeah," agreed Bianca, her tone slipping into the sarcastic, "and all you have to do is convince a race of creatures that call you God Killer it wasn't your fault."

"Piece of cake."

"We're with you, Marv," shouted Gerber. "And if the worst happens, I make you this solemn pledge – Challenge of the Unknown will stay on the air."

"You're a true friend, Maxie." Richards cut the phone connection, saying, "Son of a bitch probably wants me to lose so he can hire a new host and pay him a lot less."

"That's show biz."

"Sergeant Jones, you've been taking notes." As the detective smiled in spite of herself, Richards added, "I will, of course, be defending myself. Who's going to prosecute? Please tell me it's not one of those ex-DAs from the Crime and Punishment Channel."

"Actually, he's right outside."

Opening the office door, Bianca gestured to a dark corner. As she did, part of the blackness separated and moved forward, consolidating into a humanoid shape. The thing's 'skin' was an ebony so deep it was reflective. Its face and hands seemed to be flowing. The creature's movements as it approached appeared slow, possibly painful. Bowing in greeting, it said;

I/we ... have not names you would understand ... Since this form is here to represent my/our god, call me/us Shash

"A pleasure to meet you," said Lora, instantly regretted it.

There is no pleasure in this for any ... It is what needs be done to restore the Balance

And, so saying, Shash faded back into nothingness.

"Oh yeah," commented Richards quietly, "that son'va bitch is going to make great TV."

***

The mechanics of broadcasting into another dimension took several days to work out.

"Let me get this straight," asked Marc Thorner, Chief Engineer for Challenge. "You want me to rig a live feed into another dimension?"

When Lora assured him they were serious, the IT wizard set to work, coming up with a plan that surprised everyone else not only with its audacity, but in that it actually worked. It involved the summoning of one of Shash's fellow creatures, one that everyone collectively decided to name Buggs. Once the second shadow being permitted itself to be used as a portal through which cables, monitors and other equipment might be passed, the crew found transmission to be possible.

"How do we know they won't cheat?"

"It's been worked out, Lora," Bianca explained. "When it's time to vote, trusted psychics on our side will be linked to their watcher. An hour after closing arguments we'll have a verdict."

"And if Marv loses?"

It was the one question for which neither woman had an acceptable answer.

***

As the trial began the off-camera moderator explained that there would be no judge, nor a jury – just the participants and the cameras. As per Richards's suggestion, one to which Shash instantly concurred, the prosecution opened first.

It is agreed that the Bugg Shash, God of Gods, Giver of All, the Guiding Force of our universe, was summoned to this cold world in which I now stand, and here He died. Beyond ... it was this man, Shash pointed to Richards, his painful movements making his action appear thoughtful and dignified, *this shallow, contemptible murderer, who permitted, who arranged, who transpired for the incantation to be spoken. He is responsible for this disastrous convocation. He must restore the Balance. He must make amends*

Shash continued making his bitter points for some minutes. Richards could not help but note that the creature's communication skills had greatly improved.

"Didn't take him all that long to drop that 'I/we' nonsense." The anchorman paid strict attention to everything his prosecutor had to say. Then, when it was finally his turn to speak, he rose and faced the cameras, saying;

"As my esteemed colleague has said, Bugg Shash, who to some was a god to be adored, but to others was nothing more than a murderous beast, was summoned unto the Earthly plane of existence. As it has also been established, there he did die, a fitting and deserved death." As a thick grumble was felt coming from the shadow realm, Richards added;

"What my colleague has implied, but in no way established, however, is wherein the fault might lie for this death. I can tell you right now – frankly, and with no fear of contradiction, that this fault does not lie with myself or any of the crew of Challenge of the Unknown. Rather, it was through the arrogant negligence on the part of Bugg Shash itself that this supposed 'god' met its unexpected destruction."

At that point, per previous agreement, a video of Bugg Shash's summoning was shown. Lora had argued that replaying the death of their god might inflame the shadow dwellers, but Richards had disagreed.

"It shows what happened," he had explained. "It shows I was as surprised as anyone. It also makes some points I need made."

After the viewing, the prosecution called its first witness.

I summon the one known as Lora Dean to answer questions.

The young woman had, of course, been expecting the call – dreading it. Knowing that any wrong word might condemn her friend, Lora took the stand.

This was not the first time a show you broadcast caused deaths, was it, Lora Dean?

"No."

Explain.

Reluctantly, Lora related the story of the unfortunate leprechaun episode. When asked how many died, she related;

"There are ... unconfirmed reports of ... of several million deaths."

And the one called Richards could not have known this would happen? Seizing the opportunity to defend her boss, Lora readily agreed, prompting Shash to ask;

But afterwards, the one called Richards had to have known it could happen again.

As this was not a question, Lora did not answer. But with his point made, Shash continued, asking;

And knowing such might happen again, why did not the one called Richards first try the incantation in a smaller area, where only he would be at risk? It could have been ... Shash searched for the right human word, finally deciding upon, *... captured and shown later*

"Live TV is more dramatic."

Yes ... And more deadly

Shash withdrew and allowed Richards to cross examine.

"Ms. Dean, the book that was used, did I write it?"

"No."

"Did I find it?"

"No."

"Did I in anyway cause it to be?"

"No."

"The ritual in the book, what was its purpose? What exactly did it do?"

"It summoned Bugg Shash."

"It summoned Bugg-Shash. Thank you, Ms. Dean. The ritual summoned Bugg Shash. But, before we proceed further, perhaps we should explain a very crucial word in that sentence for our non-human viewers. What exactly does the word 'summon' mean, Ms. Dean?"

"Ah ... 'to call' or 'invite.' I mean, when those in authority 'summon' someone, it's more of a command ..."

"And do you believe me to have had any authority over Bugg-Shash?" As a wave of amusement filtered through from the shadow realm at the very idea of a human being able to command their god, Lora confirmed that such was impossible.

"So, what you're saying, Ms. Dean, is that if someone asks you to come into their home, if they indeed open the door for you and invite you in, do you have to enter?"

"No."

"And if you do enter, enter knowing that there is something inside that might kill you, might you not be responsible for your own death?"

Chaos erupted in the makeshift courtroom as a conflicted blast of pure emotion shattered its way through from the shadow realm. Before Lora could answer the question asked of her, Shash moved forward, demanding;

Tell it truly, without deception ... did you not ask the one known as Richards if he had killed a god for what you called higher ratings

The question chilled the young woman. Not only did it speak to motive but it also revealed that, as she had fearfully suspected, the shadows had been watching them even back then. Knowing they knew the truth, she admitted;

"Yes."

And what did he respond

"Mr. Richards said," Lora answered, a sob in her voice, "'Sure looks that way, don't it? Ain't it cool?'"

There was other testimony, other evidence presented and refuted by each side. Most everyone assumed, however, that Lora's last statement would be the pivot around which the trial results would turn. After several more hours, Shash conceded that he/it had said all that was needed. Thanking him, Richards then surprised everyone by turning to the cameras and announcing that he needed to call but one further witness. None were more surprised when he revealed the name of the needed party.

"Sergeant Bianca Jones."

Once the officer had taken the stand, the producer took a deep breath, held it for a moment, then finally released it and walked forward, asking as he did;

"Ms. Jones, do you like me very much?"

"No, not really."

"Still, would you lie for me? Would you try to deceive those of the shadow realm for my benefit?"

"Not for all the crabs in Baltimore."

"Very well. That thought in mind, I'm going to ask you a very important question. Our good friend Shash over here, he started all this, claiming that I had to do something. What was it he said he wanted me to do?" Bianca thought for a moment, then answered;

"He said, 'the Balance must be restored.'"

"Yes ... the balance must be restored. What do you think he meant by that?"

"I ..."

As experienced as she was in giving testimony, the sergeant suddenly realized she was being lead somewhere. The anchorman had already revealed he did not expect her to lie for him. As time divided into split seconds within her head, Bianca's mind raced. She did not necessarily want to see the producer dead, did not want to risk an inter-dimensional war. Realizing her hesitation had gone too far, she said;

"I don't actually know. I'd been assuming Shash's people wanted you dead. But ... no ... that would 'create' a new balance ... not restore an old one ..."

Come on, gorgeous, thought Richards, his years of on-camera time keeping his true emotions from showing on his face. It's been there right in front of us the whole time. You can do it ... you can do it ...

"I can't say for certain what Shash might have meant, you understand," the sergeant said slowly, watching Richards closely as she spoke. "But, to restore something means to make it as it once was. To reestablish the status quo ...”

“Exactly,” snapped the anchorman, cutting Bianca off before she went any further. Having gotten out into the open what he needed, Richards poured the most sympathetic vocal honey he possessed into his voice as he turned to the cameras to explain;

“Our viewers on the other side may not know this, but there are words one cannot say on network television. They are what humans refer to as ‘dirty’ words. Tonight I am going to break a rule. I am going to say a word that may not have been officially designated as offensive, but which far too many in this modern age have come to be regard as dirty. Disgusting. Heinous. It outlines a concept few people believe in. And that word is ...” Richards paused for effect, then thundered;

“Responsibility!”

As Bianca smiled, the anchorman became a highly animated story-teller as he spewed;

“People ... they don’t want it – they won’t take it. Back during that leprechaun business mentioned earlier, those who died when a man named Delroney tempted humanity with a tale of gold and riches, they died not because I gave him a stage from which to present his tale ... they died because of greed. And when Bugg Shash was summoned unto this plane of existence, he died for the same reason.”

Throughout the room, around the globe, in every corner of the shadow realm, all attention fixed itself upon Marvin Richards. Sitting back in her chair, relaxing as she settled into the realization that the anchorman knew what he was doing, Bianca smiled in honest admiration as Richards shouted;

“Bugg-Shash accepted an invitation to visit another dimension, and came roaring in with murder in its heart. As it had done so many times before. And for its reckless greed, it was destroyed, its atoms scattered beyond its ability to recover them.” Spinning around then, Richards stabbed a finger at Shash, demanding;

“Tell me, we might have summoned your god, but could it not have refused to come?”

I ... I/we ... suppose

“Because, if it could not have refused, it could not have been a god – correct?”

As Shash waved its arms helplessly, Richards paused long enough to fill his eyes with his most practiced sincerity, then turned back to the camera, announcing;

"Responsibility. On both sides, in both worlds, we are all of us ... responsible. For the death of a god, for the upsetting of a natural balance. This must be redressed. Payment must be made. There can be no denying, my good friend Shash here is utterly correct ... the Balance must be restored."

Walking over to the other side of the room, Richards stood before the representative of the Shadow world, then said;

"Shash. Your god is dead. On behalf of myself, my crew, my network and all the people of Earth, I offer you a new one."

You ... you would become our god

"No, I would replace it. But heed me. The god I offer is a jealous god – one that demands its followers' full attention, one that both controls their lives and enriches them. It is a god meant to be worshipped daily, hourly. Constantly. But, for all that, it offers an escape from life's cares and troubles. It brings peace and tranquility, and refreshingly in every way makes one's world better and better."

Putting his arm around Shash, every ounce of his demeanor meant to convey wisdom and benevolence, Richards slowly turned the shadow creature around to face the camera, then whispered;

"Behold the face of your new god."

***

"I don't believe it," laughed Bianca after Shash had accepted Richards's offer and departed, "Television? You gave them television as a god?"

"Why not, Sergeant? In every corner of this world where people don't murder each other over the proper pronunciation of their deity's name, it's the only god most people have."

As Bianca shook her head sadly, no longer hating Richards as a person, but reaffirming her long-standing rule to never allow media people of any manner to infiltrate her life, the producer said;

"Oh, I'll admit there're still problems to be worked out – how to transmit a signal? How to charge for programming?"

"Let alone deciding on content," interjected Lora.

"God, yes," agreed Richards. "I've been thinking at first we send them nothing but sci fi movies in which Earth kicks alien butt. Work on making an impression that keeps them on their side of the portal. And most importantly, there's the research needed to find out exactly what they have over there, and what they don't. And how to convince them that they need what they don't have."

"After all," smiled Lora, "what's TV without commercials?"

"God," laughed Bianca, "I really should have gone with my first thought and kicked your ass out of Baltimore. Instead I helped you begin the seduction and commercialization of an entire dimension."

"What you did, Ms. Jones, was to help save this one. But you are correct, Sergeant, their universe is now forever changed."

"Poor bastards," said Bianca. "First we kill their god and soon we'll be taking their souls."

"That is show biz," sighed Lora. "The maw that requires constant feeding."

"Why, yes," said Richards, throwing his words out as if they had just occurred to him, and not as if he had been holding them to the ready, waiting for the right moment to release them.

"And with that thought in mind, Sergeant, where exactly is this disappearing house I've heard so much about?"

A CHOICE OF DAMNATIONS

It was just past six in the morning when George Lanvale felt the cold barrel of a rifle pressed against his neck.

"Not a sound, Mr. Lanvale. Your wife and children are safe, for now. If you want them to remain in that condition you will quietly get out of bed and follow my instructions."

I must still be asleep, Lanvale thought, but the metal on his skin felt too real. He turned away from the gun, moving slowly just in case.

Not a dream. The open end of some sort of rifle was inches from his face. A tall, white-haired man stood over him.

"Use the bathroom, brush your teeth, get dressed," ordered the man. "This gun is meant to demonstrate that I mean business but any resistance on your part will mean pain for your family."

Still dreaming, Lanvale hoped, knowing he wasn't. Leaving the bathroom door open he emptied his bladder and cleaned his teeth in full view of the invader. Still dazed, he put on jeans and a polo shirt and was led downstairs.

Emily, Samantha and Eric were in the living room. The frightened children were crying, Sam trying and failing to be brave for her younger brother. Emily wanted to reach out to them but was prevented by one of the four men who had taken over the house. Unlike the one with the rifle, the others were masked and carried nasty looking handguns.

Lanvale was not a timid man or a stupid one. No one had been hurt yet. They want something, he reasoned. "Who are you? What do you want?" he asked the white-blonde man.

He was answered with a smile and "A fair question and an expected one. One that deserves an answer. Who I am, who we are, is not important. When the time comes the police may or may not figure it out. As to what we want, what I want, that is simple, Mr. Lanvale. I want you to kill as many people as possible."

"That's ..."

"Ridiculous, impossible, crazy? Possibly all of those things, Mr. Lanvale. And next I expect you to say that I cannot expect you to and that I will not get away with whatever I am planning. Well, it is likely that ultimately I will not get away it. There is, after all, a price for the choices we make. But I do expect you to do exactly what I say."

The man motioned Lanvale to sit down. Handing his rifle to one of the masked men, he joined him.

"I have brought brutal men into your home, Mr. Lanvale. Unless you follow my orders I will turn them loose on your family. There is nothing that they will not do to them. Your wife, son and daughter will suffer horribly before being killed. Or maybe they won't be killed. Maybe they'll be left alive, crippled in mind and body, reliving this day over and over all the while knowing that you could have prevented it."

"What do you want me to do?"

"My … associates have filled your car with sufficient explosives to take down a small building. In," the man looked at his watch, "two hours you will leave here and drive your car into the city. You are fifteen minutes from downtown Baltimore. Once there you will pick a suitable target and, using the remote you will find on your front seat, detonate the explosives."

Not a dream but a nightmare, one for which he was fully awake. Unable to believe what was happening Lanvale's mind shut down for a moment then restarted in fear and confusion. Questions demanded to be asked; so many that none would come out. Finally Lanvale forced out the most obvious one.

"If I … I do what you say? What happens to my family?"

He knew the answer, they'd be killed but not tortured, a small mercy. Instead he heard,

"No harm will come to them, beyond the terror of this day of course. But physically they will not be touched. It may mean nothing to you but I give you my word on that."

"And how do I know you'll keep your word?"

"Another fair question. You, Mr. Lanvale, are being asked to choose between your family and total strangers. Three people who mean the world to you versus dozens, maybe hundreds, of those whose lives mean nothing to you. You are the first to whom I am giving this choice."

Pausing, the man let Lanvale consider his words.

"If I kill your family, the next man or woman to be offered this choice will reject it, reject me. He or she must be assured that I will do what I say. Your story, told to the police and media and repeated endlessly on the Internet, will be that assurance. If you do what I ask, if you choose to save your family, they will know that they can save theirs. If you decide to save strangers, then the sufferings of your loved ones will presage what will happen to theirs."

The man was crazy, he had to be. This was some kind of elaborate hoax, a reality show gone bad. Somewhere there had to be hidden cameras and a crazed producer. Looking up, Lanvale studied the face of the one next to him. The white-blonde man permitted it, permitted him to stare through his eyes and into his soul. What Lanvale saw there was sincerity, peace and the utter conviction that what he was doing what absolutely the right and proper thing.

There was no reality show. Nor was this madness, not as Lanvale understood it. Looking at his family, thinking of the faceless, unknown dead, George Lanvale made his choice.

"What's the target?"

"City Hall, Police Headquarters, the Harbor tunnel, a school would be nice but I do not expect that, not from you. It is your choice, Mr. Lanvale. All that I ask is sizeable property damage and a sufficient death toll. If I hear of that occurring by nine-thirty this morning, your family will be safe, from me at least."

Again the man looked at his watch. "We have some time, spend it with your family."

As Lanvale gathered his wife and children to him, Emily spoke for the first time.

"Why are you doing this?"

A shrug. "To free the oppressed peoples of Palestine, to bring terror to America, to strike at the heart of the Great Satan, to protest the financial hold the US has on the rest of the world, for the greater glory of the Bright One. All of these reasons, none of them. Take your pick. In reality, I'm doing it because I can."

Ninety minutes later, the white-blonde man led Lanvale to his explosive laden sedan.

"By the way, Mr. Lanvale, The remote will operate up to 75 yards away. You do not have to be in your car when it explodes. You can die with your victims or live to be with your family, though if you survive I'm sure neither the police nor the federal government will allow you much time with them. Either way, it's your choice and you can live or die with it."

My choice, thought Lanvale. I could choose to end it now. Press the button and this man and I both die now.

As if in answer to Lanvale's thoughts, the man said, "By now your family is in the basement. The blast would not kill them. My men, however, would take them away before the police came. They would be days, possibly weeks dying. Remember, Mr. Lanvale. Property damage, and a death toll or I turn my men loose."

Driving towards downtown, George Lanvale tried to decide who should die. What should he destroy, how many deaths would save his family? On Harford Road he drove past a funeral procession. "Not enough," something told him. Belair Road had banks and supermarkets. Lots of savers and shoppers. The Northeast District Police Station was not too far. Drive up to the door and blow it up, save civilian lives.

He could just drive to the district and tell them what happened. Could they respond in time to save his family? Would they? Could he take that chance?

Now on North Avenue heading west. The Eastside Court Building maybe. Lanvale drove by it, doubted if he could get his car close enough to kill enough people.

From North Avenue Lanvale turned onto I-83 towards downtown. And stopped. An accident had stalled traffic. Stuck on an elevated road surrounded by other drivers, he was running out of time. Fate and circumstances had made his choice for him. Praying to God for his family's safety and his own salvation, George Lanvale picked up the remote and pressed the button.

News of the I-83 collapse preempted all local Baltimore channels, then went national as the reason for the collapse became evident.

"Your husband made a wise choice, Mrs. Lanvale. You and your family have my sympathies, both for your loss and for what you are about to endure. It won't be long before hordes of government men are swarming over your home. They will not believe you at first. But I promise, they will soon."

The white-blonde man signaled his men to leave. As they did so, he carefully placed a glass from which he had been drinking on the coffee table.

"Be sure to point this out to them," was the last thing he said before leaving the house.

Five minutes went by, then ten as a stunned Emily Lanvale waited for the men to return and finish what they had started. When it became clear that they would not, she called the police.

***

The 911 call came in as a home invasion. An officer responded within ten minutes. On hearing that armed men had somehow broken in and terrorized the family, he immediately called for a robbery detective and the crime lab to respond. He then tried to get a statement from the sobbing woman.

Emily Lanvale had tried to be brave, to not break down in front of her children and to give the police the information she knew they should have. But her husband was dead, had died saving her and her children, buying their lives with the deaths of many innocent people. Part of her was glad that he had, glad that her children were safe and unharmed. Another part felt the weight of those killed, a survivor's guilt that would stay with her for the rest of her life.

When the officer arrived at her door looking younger than George had on the day they first met, she broke down. Hysterical, all she managed to tell him through her tears and cries was that men with guns had broken in.

Samantha Lanvale knew something was wrong, very wrong. Bad men had come in and scared them all. They had taken her father and a policeman had come and her mother was crying. She remembered the white-haired man saying something about a bomb, and the man on TV was talking about a bomb. And there was something about a glass.

Pulling her mother's sleeve, Samantha pointed to the glass then to the TV. "Tell them about the bomb, Mommy."

Detectives from the Homicide Unit arrived shortly after. By then the crime scene tech had taken all her photographs, dusted any surfaces the invaders might have touched and was trying to figure out how they had gotten into the house.

She had just decided on the kitchen door as being the probable point of entry when a detective called to her.

"Anything, Tammy?"

Tammy Dolan looked up from examining the door lock. "Some scratches that might be from a pick. I'll take the lock just in case."

Detective Bethany Steele nodded. "What about the glass?"

"Swabbed for DNA and dusted. Got some good prints, almost too good, as if they'd been left deliberately."

"If you believe Ms. Lanvale they probably were."

"Do we believe Ms. Lanvale?"

"I was skeptical at first, Tammy. She might have made it up to cover for a crazy husband."

"But …"

"Once we got her calmed down Ms. Lanvale said that the one in charge, the white haired guy who wasn't masked, said something about 'the Bright One.'"

"The same Bright One that witch on Evergreen said she worshipped?"

"Know any other Bright Ones?"

"Oh shit."

"Oh shit indeed. We better call Bianca."

***

Sergeant Bianca Jones was assigned to the Baltimore Police Department's Special Operations Unit. It was her responsibility to investigate those cases that did not fit neatly into any other category. The strange, the weird, the unexplained and the unimaginable all came across her desk. In most cases the incidents had mundane causes and perfectly rational explanations. Bianca was authorized to handle those that did not in any manner she saw fit, including the use of lethal force. She was answerable only to the Police Commissioner and he seldom questioned her methods. It was her job to keep the city safe from extraordinary threats. It was one she did very well.

Bianca was alone in her office when her phone rang.

"Jones here."

"Bianca, Beth." Beth Steele quickly explained the situation.

"'The greater glory of the Bright One.' Those were his exact words?"

"He spouted some crap about other causes but how would he know about the Bright One?"

"He shouldn't," Bianca said more to herself than to Beth. No one should know except the few people she regarded as her teammates and those involved with Delilah Solomon.

Solomon had been a self-styled witch who had used threats of dark magic to terrorize her neighborhood. When Bianca confronted her, the witch had called on the powers of this Bright One. It had done her little good. Solomon had not survived the confrontation. No mention of the Bright One was made in any of the heavily censored reports.

But now the name was connected to a bombing in the city.

Like most city cops, Bianca didn't trust Federal officers. She had good cause. In one encounter, they had seized all evidence from the scene of a multiple murder in a futile attempt at a cover-up, but not before

Bianca had threatened to shoot two of them.

"Give me the address, Beth. And don't notify the Feds until I get there."

"Too late on that, Bianca. Some sergeant's already made the call."

"Tell Tammy to finish up now. I don't want her there when the Feds arrive."

Once Tammy's evidence was submitted it would be harder for the Feds to get. They would have to go through channels and paperwork had a habit of getting lost or misdirected. By the time it reached them the BPD Crime Lab would have done its work.

Breaking the connection, Bianca looked down at her desk. The sarcophagus missing from the Walters Art Gallery and the threats against the city's fortune tellers would have to wait. The bombing case was more important. Saying a silent prayer that she was wrong and that it would prove to be nothing more than what it appeared, she set out, but not before checking her pistol. One never knew when one might have to shoot a Fed.

By the time Bianca got to the scene the Lanvale's house was surrounded by very serious men and women wearing black combat vests over business suits and carrying impressive automatic weapons. The few BPD officers remaining on the scene were gathered on the sidewalk or at the edge of the lawn waiting for the order to secure.

As Bianca pulled up, Beth Steele came over to her. "You wasted a trip, Bianca. About ten minutes after I called you the men in black showed up and took over the investigation in the name of national security. Then they threw us off our own crime scene."

"Tammy get away okay?"

Beth nodded. "I told her not to go back to the Lab until she had everything written up and then to go straight to Evidence Control. To tell you the truth, those guys are so interested in looking for bombs, browbeating Mrs. Lanvale, and scaring the kids I don't think they've noticed. Hey, where you going? They told us to stay out."

"They told you to stay out, Beth."

Bianca moved slowly up the walk, so as not to startle anyone. She didn't want to start a shooting was between agencies, especially not with her in the middle. As she approached, she knew what the agents guarding the house were seeing and thinking. A small, slender young woman, no bigger than a teen, was coming towards them. Whoever she was, she had somehow talked her way past the local cops. Whoever she was, she was going to be sent on her way PDQ.

"Sorry, honey," said an agent whose vest had the stitched name Delroy. "The Lanvales don't need no babysitting today."

Bianca smiled. She was used to being taken for granted due to her size. She had never liked it, but she was used to it. Sometime it proved useful. For instance, by not seeing her as a threat Agent Delroy had allowed her to get close enough to take his weapon and shove it down his throat if she wanted. Tempting as that idea was, she reminded herself that she didn't want to start any unnecessary trouble. Instead she carefully removed her ID from her coat pocket.

"Sergeant Bianca Jones, Special Ops, BPD. I'd like to speak with the Agent-in-Charge."

Delroy gave her the expected "You're a cop?" look then said officiously, "In case your co-workers didn't tell you, Sergeant, this scene is now under Federal jurisdiction. I'm going to have to ask you leave the property."

There were several things Bianca could have done. There was a name she could drop which would have gotten her inside the house. There was a call she could make that would have accomplished the same thing. She could have simply walked by Delroy and dared him to shoot a BPD Sergeant.

She did none of these. Instead she gave a somewhat theatrical sigh and said, "It was worth a try." Handing Delroy a business card she added, "At your earliest convenience please give this to the AIC and tell him that I had information relevant to his investigation but that you refused to allow me to see him."

With another smile and a "Have a nice day, hon," Bianca hurried from the scene, apparently not hearing Agent Delroy calling her name. Gesturing Beth into her car, Bianca drove away.

"We're now on record as having tried to cooperate. We can do our thing while they do theirs."

Beth did not look happy. "You know, Bianca, this isn't a game. Believe it or not, we're all on the same side. Those guys back there might be over the top, holier than thou assholes, but they want to catch the terrorists as much as we do. Why not cooperate?"

"Who said we're not, or rather, I'm not? The evidence from the scene is secure with a proper chain of custody. We've given them all the help they asked for."

"Which is none."

"Granted, but whose fault is that? And when their AIC calls me and asks for my relevant information I'll tell him all about Delilah Solomon and the Bright One."

"A witch and a terrorist. He won't believe you."

"He will, but not until it happens again."

***

Two days later Howard Ray made the mistake of resisting the men who had broken into his home. Broken and bleeding, but not dying – the invaders made sure of that – the man with the white-blonde hair explained things to his family.

"Any more resistance and you will all die horribly over several days. As I was saying, despite what you may have heard on the news, I was responsible for the I-83 bombing. The poor unfortunate who detonated the bomb did so at my bidding. He did it to save his family. One of you today will be given the same choice as he was. Kill innocents or your family will suffer greatly then die. Since Mr. Ray is in no condition to participate, the decision falls to …"

He looked at Sarah the mother. No, she worked better as a hostage. The two younger girls were just that, too young. That left …

"To you, young man. Your name is Douglas, is it not?"

Douglas Ray nodded. He was just seventeen and more scared than he'd ever been in his life. It was taking all he had to not wet the front of his jeans in fear. And now this stranger was handing him a gun.

"Yes, it is loaded. And yes, you could try to shoot me and my men. You would get one shot off and then you would die. So would your family, eventually. Take the gun and hold it down by your side."

Douglas obeyed.

"Very good. Now I want you to go someplace crowded and kill as many people as you can before you are stopped. It doesn't matter where. You can choose."

"What if I don't? What if I just go to the cops?"

The white-blonde man took Douglas aside. "That is your choice, one which will certainly save many lives including your own. But if you do," his voice dropped to a whisper only Douglas could hear, "I'll start with your mother. When I'm done with her my men will rape her repeatedly. Then we will do the same to your sisters. And when we are finished, we will break several bones in each of their bodies and do it all over again. We will let your father watch. We will let them all know that you could have prevented their suffering but did not." Stepping away he said aloud, "It's your choice."

No one expects to die in a grocery store, not even in Baltimore. On that day eight people did. Four more were wounded, all at the hand of a scared teenager who wanted to protect his family. The store's security guard was old and slow and would always regret not being able to save those eight lives. However, he would not regret firing the bullet that took the life of Douglas Ray and ended his killing spree.

When the news of the tragic shootings at the Food Fair broke, the white-blonde signaled his men that it was time to leave.

"Mrs. Douglas, my condolences on the death of your son. Mr. Douglas, had it not been for your foolish resistance, your son would not be dead. I hope you can live with your choice..."

As he left, the man carefully left the glass from which he had been drinking water on the dining room table around which the Douglas Family had been sitting.

***

The connection was not made until the police interviewed family of the late Douglas Ray. The standing orders having already been issued, Bianca Jones was called right away. With her husband on his way to the hospital, Sarah was the one questioned.

"This blonde-haired man, did he or anyone mentioned his name."

"N-no," Sarah stammered. She did not want to be there. She wanted to be with her husband. She wanted to see her dead son one more time. She wanted to lie to her daughters and tell them that everything was going to be all right. Yet she knew that her place right then was with the police, telling them what they needed to know to catch this madman.

"No," she repeated. "No one else t-talked, only him. He touched that." She indicated the glass on the table.

"One more question, Ms. Ray," Bianca said gently. "Did this man say anything about the Bright One?"

A shake of Sarah's head was her answer.

"We're done for now. Your daughters are with your neighbors. Would you like someone to drive you to the hospital?"

A nod this time.

"I'll arrange that. Don't be surprised if some Federal cops have some questions for you – lots of questions."

"If anything," Bianca said to Beth Steele after Sarah Ray left, "this should get the Feds to stop thinking of the Lanvales as a terrorist cell. I'm heading back."

"What about the scene?"

Bianca shrugged. "Leave it for the Feds. We're cooperating, remember?" She looked at the drinking glass. "It's not like we don't know that the prints and DNA will match. Whatever his reasons, this guy wants us to know it's him."

***

Two hours later, this became evident to all when a video was posted on the Internet and released to all major media outlets.

It was shot from the speaker's POV and it showed first the Lanvales then the Rays. The audience heard what the families had heard and learned of the hard choices that had been made. News footage of the I-83 bombing and the Food Fair killings followed. Then the releases of the surviving families were shown.

"We are agents of He Who is to Come," came a voiceover. "Your choices will prove your worth. People of Baltimore, decide now how you will choose when it is your turn."

Police Commissioner Williams swore as he turned off the video. "Son of a bitch had a camera. Damn it, Jones, I thought we were supposed to be safe from this sort of thing."

"Only from the One Below, Sir. This one looks homegrown."

"Do you think this Bright One you're worried about is 'He Who is to Come?'"

"Could be, Sir. If it is and he shows up we should be ready for him. We've got enough resources to take down a god."

"Right now I'll settle for you stopping a terrorist."

"What about the Feds?"

"They're moving in. They've already taken over most of the fifth floor. They want the city under martial law – armed troops patrolling the street, dusk to dawn curfew, cameras on every corner. The mayor and governor have resisted, so far. But there's fear that this thing will spread."

"It will if marital law is declared. These guys will only go somewhere else."

"You think so?"

"It's what I would do, Commissioner."

The BPD's top cop stood and looked out the windows of his corner office. Half of the city was in view.

"We've had fires, riots, demons in the street and the worst blizzards on record. Baltimore doesn't deserve this. Stop them for me, Bianca, however you can. I'll deal with the Feds; give them men, money, whatever they need. You work separately from them. They don't believe your 'Bright One' story anyway. They've never heard of him."

"No one has, Sir. If there is a connection, it's the most secret society ever."

"Then how do we stop them?"

"The usual way – solid police work and we pray for a break."

***

For the longest time, Zachary Knox had had little enjoyment in life. He woke up, got dressed, went to work, came home, ate dinner, watched TV and went to bed. For five days a week that was his routine, except for Wednesday night. That was the night he and the wife skipped late night TV, went to bed early and, as his wife would say, "had relations." Neither Knox nor his wife took much joy in the act. For him it was some mild pleasure and a release of tension. And while he never asked, Knox suspected that his wife did it because that was what wives were expected to do. Both would probably have been happier watching The Tonight Show.

Weekends were yard work and home repairs on Saturday and sports on Sunday. Knox liked sports, it didn't matter what game or what team. Sports were interesting, and something to do until bedtime and for the week's cycle to start all over.

One Tuesday morning a white-blonde man changed all that. Knox was herded into his living room by a hooded man with a gun. There he found his family being guarded by other hooded men with guns and an unmasked man.

Sipping from a glass of water, the white-blonde man explained things. As Knox listened to his choices he looked over at his family. His wife of seventeen years was unattractive, only a fair cook and lousy in the sack. His children – the boy sixteen, the girl fifteen – were C students at best, not good at sports, and likely to work minimum wage jobs all their lives. It did not occur to him that any of this might be his fault.

What did occur to him was that he valued their lives less than his own and equal to that of the strangers he was being asked to kill.

"Do you understand the choice you have to make, Mr. Knox?"

Knox was staring at his wife when the white-blond asked this question. As she realized what his choice would be Knox saw true emotions cross her face for the first time in many years. Fear, despair, the promise that if they all survived things would be better.

For you, maybe, he thought. I'll be in little pieces inside a collapsing, flooding tunnel.

"Yes, I do," he told the unmasked man. Calmly taking the keys to car loaded with explosives, he left his family without a goodbye or a backward glance.

Knox drove directly to the Southwest Police District.

In the living room, a cellular receiver hidden in the car broadcasted Knox's comments to the police to his family and the armed men.

"The terrorists, the ones on TV, they're in my house. There's a bomb in this car. The car is a bomb."

As police shouted "Get out of the car" and "what's your address" and "call QRT" the white-blonde man shut off the speaker.

"It had to happen sooner or later," he said to no one in particular. "Still, I thought it would have taken longer." To Zachary Knox's family he said, "It's a pity you didn't love each other more."

On standby for just such an incident, it took the BPD Quick Response Team five minutes to roll out, ten minutes to get to the Knox home and only three to learn that no one was there. Now working together, a crime scene team made up of Federal and local forensic experts found no useful evidence other than a drinking glass from which latent prints and possible DNA were recovered.

A glad-to be-alive Zachary Knox did not add anything to what the investigators already knew about the terrorists. The over five hour interview ended badly when Det. McLarney of BPD Homicide asked, "Why did you do it, Mr. Knox? Why did you risk your family like that?"

Expecting an answer such as "I thought they were bluffing," everyone in the room was shocked when Know replied, "To tell you the truth, I never liked them all that much anyway."

Most of those that didn't want to shoot him wanted to beat the crap out of him. A city cop who'd just gone through a bitter divorce and a Fed who had just dumped an abusive boyfriend understood and wondered what they would have done in his place.

***

Three days later the video hit the Internet. In it, Bryan Knox was shown being savagely beaten. Then, his body bruised, his face bloodied, his limbs twisted and broken, masked men repeatedly forced themselves on him. When they had finished with him, as Bryan lay moaning in agony, covered with his assailants' waste and fluids, the camera pulled back to show that his mother and sister had been present the entire time.

"Happy with your choice, Mrs. Knox?" The off camera voice was calm, almost gentle. As the camera zoomed in the dying boy's mother the voice continued.

"I suppose you thought there was less that we could do to your son than to your daughter. That he might suffer less. And now you know you were wrong. Still, it might be of some comfort to you that you spared your daughter the same fate."

Some unseen signal was given. A single shot was heard and the young girl standing next to Connie Knox fell dead.

"As agreed, Mrs. Knox, your daughter is free. Free from the memory of her father's betrayal, free from witnessing her brother's ordeal, free from life itself. That doesn't mean we won't be abusing her corpse. But that's for later. Now it's your turn."

They took twice as long with the mother, and did far worse. When it was over, as she lay next to the now still body of her son, the calm, gentle voice said,

"Zachary Knox had a choice. To save you he chose this." The camera panned over the bodies of the dead and dying. "One day all will have to choose. Choose between friend and stranger. Choose between family and friend. Choose between son and daughter, mother and father, sister and brother."

A fast-forward reply of the tortures of Connie and Bryan Knox began to play as the voice continued.

"Soon the Bright One, He Who is to Come, will announce His Presence. Choose wisely and be safe. Choose not and be hunted. Choose poorly and not a sin will be left uncommitted on those you love."

***

"There's nothing your team can do?"

Bianca Jones shook her head. "There's still no word on who or what this 'Bright One' is. Knox's car was clean. No hits on the prints or DNA from any of the scenes. Maybe when, if we find the bodies ..."

Frustrated, tired to the point of exhaustion, Bianca slumped back in her chair. "A break's got to come." She said this as more as a prayer than with any sense of confidence.

"Does it? How many are going to die, either that way," the Commissioner pointed to the now blank video screen, "or blown up and shot when the next target chooses his family over public safety. Dammit, Sergeant, we have to make our own breaks."

"We're doing all we can, Sir. Homicide, the Crime Lab, the district detectives, uniforms – everyone's working sixteen on and eight off patrolling the streets and running down leads. Plus Homeland Security's moved in and locked up anyone with any possible connection to terrorism."

"And all that's accomplished is to inflame every minority and most of the religious groups in the city. What about tracing these monsters through – other means? Has that been tried?"

"So far they're not a magical threat so the Department of Mystic Affairs can't get involved. And the FBI and Homeland Security don't believe in magic."

"The FBI didn't believe in the Mafia and look where that got them. What about your husband?"

Bianca's husband, Joe Russo, had once been a crime scene specialist for the BPD Crime Lab. Injured in the line of duty, he retired and took over Morgan's Rare Books and Collectibles after the death of its owner. In addition to the shop, Joe had inherited a sizeable library of arcane and dangerous books on magic and the supernatural. As he became familiar with these books, Joe developed an affinity for certain kinds of magic.

Bianca side-stepped the question. "There's nothing in his books."

"That's not what I asked, Sergeant."

Bianca knew what the Commissioner meant. He wanted Joe to attempt to find the terrorist through magic. The problem was that Joe was not an expert and the one he would be tracking just might be. The odds were good that any spell Joe cast could be traced back to him.

The young sergeant could imagine what might happen next. Joe would be taken and Bianca would be confronted with a choice no one should have to make. Joe's life or the lives of innocents. She knew which choice Joe would want her to make. She knew what choice she should make. She did not know what choice she would make.

Not prepared to lose the only good thing in her life, she framed her reply carefully.

"Joe's kind of magic is … limited against what we're facing."

"White magic?"

Had the situation not been so dire, Bianca might have smiled at her boss's simplification. Instead all she said was, "Something like that."

"Then we might need to bring in someone … darker."

"That road, once taken, is difficult to leave."

"We may have to."

Bianca stood. "That is something I cannot be party to … Sir."

Frowning at the insubordination, the Commissioner asked harshly, "What makes you think you have any say in matter?"

Bianca's badge hit the desk.

As the shiny metal shield lay between them the two cops stared at each other. For a moment Bianca thought that Williams was going to pick it up. For a moment so did he. Finally,

"Pick that up and get back to work. Let's find these bastards before the Feds burn down the city to save it."

"Yes, Sir."

Her badge back in her pocket Bianca turned to leave. Williams called her back.

"Oh, Sergeant."

"Yes, Sir?"

"That that only works once, understood?"

"Understood, Sir."

***

A few days later came the four words everyone was waiting to hear. "We got a break."

Criminalist Tammy Dolan called Bianca with the news – someone had gotten careless while handling the C4 explosive that had been loaded into Zachary Knox's car. A thumbprint had been raised and identified. Not to any known terrorist but to a dealer out of Wilmington, North Carolina who specialized in providing guns, ammunition and other lethal items to whomever had the right amount of cash.

None too gently, the dealer was "persuaded" to give up the name of his middleman in Arlington, Virginia. He in turn was similarly convinced to provide the location where the explosives were delivered. He could not, however, give the Feds a name.

"A storage place off Belair Road," was all he could tell them. "When I got the money I dropped off the goods. Left the key to the unit someplace they could find it. That's all I did."

Given the date and time investigators viewed the storage center's security video until they saw hooded men load the deadly material into a van with blacked out plates and drive off.

"That's it then," said Agent Jack Delroy. "No faces. No plates on what's probably a stolen van. Back to square one."

"You give up too fast."

"Oh, and what would you do, Detective Steele?"

Bethany Steele was one of the BPD's representatives on what was now known as the Bright One Task Force. The Commissioner had tried to get Bianca appointed but Agent-in-Charge Charles Guthrie wanted no part of what he called "that bitch who runs the freak show."

"I don't know about the rest of you, but I worked patrol for several years before becoming a detective. If on patrol I saw a car, SUV or van without plates, I'd pull it over."

Beth paused, waited for someone to ask "So?"

"So," she said in a tone that suggested she was instructing a group of rookies on proper police procedure, "as careful as this bunch has been, they probably stopped somewhere to replace their plates. And there's a dog grooming shop just before you get to Belair Road with a perfect place to pull in at night. It also has a state of the art surveillance system. And before anyone asks how I know this, last night I went out there and looked."

A square plastic case hit the table. "That's a copy of the shop's video. It shows two hooded men putting plates on a van. The plates are quite readable and yes, I already ran them."

"Stolen? Right?"

"Believe it or not, Agent Delroy, no. They come back to a nice old lady in a somewhat run-down condo complex on Romeo Lane. That's also off Belair Road and about a ten minute drive from the storage center. It's a place that's mostly seniors and it's old. Their security system consists of bright lights that work half the time and management hoping nothing bad happens. My guess, one of our friends in the hoodies took the plates, used them on the van for the drive down Belair Road and got them back on Mrs. Ronalds's car before she knew they were gone."

"Anything else, Detective Steele?" asked Guthrie, sure that there would be and wondering how he could steal the homicide detective away from the BPD.

"What do you think? I had our crime lab go out and dust the plates, back and front. She didn't find any prints of course, our friends no doubt wiped them down, but Technician Dolan is very thorough. She also dusted the bumpers, fenders, lights and anywhere someone might have touched when putting on or taking off the plates."

Enjoying the spotlight, Beth made them wait for a moment then,

"One print from the bumper to the left of the front plate. We're running it through AFIS now."

A half hour later, Tammy Dolan texted Beth a name.

"We've got a hit. Luis Withers, lives off Coldspring in north Baltimore."

"Good job, Detective, both you and that crime lab tech."

"Thank you, sir. Not bad for a couple of bitches from the Freak Show."

A judge was found, a warrant signed. An ops team was readied within two hours of Withers being identified.

The team was made up of Detective Steele, Lieutenant Tavon Greggs of the BPD's Quick Response Team, three agents from the task force and a Federal SWAT teamed trained in anti-terrorist tactics.

They assembled on the parking lot of the Northern District Station at three a.m. At four they hit the house, shooting in teargas and flashbangs before breaking down both doors at once.

After clearing the first and second floors they found Withers in the basement, hanging from an exposed beam.

Someone pointed out the obvious.

"He's dead."

"Not for very long." Detective Steele felt the body. "Still warm."

No one had to say it, there had been a leak. That much was obvious. Who and how was not. Beth looked over the team that had hit the house. Other than Greggs she didn't know or trust any of them. And right then she was not that sure about Greggs.

"You guys get out of here. I'll call in some uniforms. We'll handle it as a regular suicide. Your boss will have my report in the morning."

Beth waited for them to leave, then she called Bianca.

***

Bianca learned the details of the raid over drinks at Frank's Hall, a popular cop bar. "That many people, there had to be a leak."

Beth shook her head. "The raiding party didn't know where they were going until the go time. By then the target was already dead."

"Someone on the task force then."

"But why? None of them seem …"

"Same reason as George Lanvale and Douglas Ray, Beth. Imagine someone calling you, telling you all about your family, where they are, what they're doing. He brings up the Knox video. Then he tells you what you need to do to keep your family safe. What would you do?"

The homicide cop thought for a moment and finally said, "Dammit, I don't really know. And it could be more than one of them. That's bad."

After a waiter brought another round Bianca smiled and said, "No, Beth, that's good. Now we've got a chance to nail these bastards."

"The Feds are probably already working on it."

"They won't move fast enough, that's why we have to."

Bianca outlined her plan.

"We're gambling with people's lives here."

"We do that every day, Beth. Let's hope the cards fall in our favor."

"The Freak Show?" Bianca said on the way out of the bar. "Not sure I like that."

"You may not have any choice. You know how these things tend to stick."

***

The task force met again early the next morning. This time there were uninvited guests. Just as the various members were sitting down Lieutenant Greggs and his QRT team burst in with weapons drawn. Bianca Jones followed them in and started speaking before anyone could speak or object.

"For those of you who don't me, I'm Sergeant Bianca Jones. One of you is helping the terrorists."

"How dare you?" protested Agent Guthrie. "You just can't …"

"I already have. And I dare because no one else will. Now one by one you will all stand for a search. I want your iPhones, BlackBerrys, Pocket Cops and whatever else one or more of you used to tip off the bad guys."

"Not without a warrant."

"Screw your warrants, Delroy. We all know that none of this is gonna end in a trial. Now give them over."

"It won't work, Sergeant Jones. All of our devices are password protected. If your computer forensics people try to hack them all they'll do is wipe the memories."

There wasn't much about her job that Bianca found funny but on hearing Guthrie's comments she could not help but laugh.

"You guys really don't pay attention, do you? I – hunt – monsters. And I use whatever means I have to – fair or foul, legal or illegal, science or magic – to do my job. I'm not going to turn your devices over to some techno-geek to play with for a week or three. I'm giving them to a magician who in a matter of hours will learn which one was used with evil intent."

During her speech, Bianca ignored the fact that most of the captive task force had their devices on their laps and were furtively texting for help. She allowed it. She had counted on it. She watched and waited. As she had hoped, one of them turned pale and started to rise.

"It's Delroy!"

The shooting started.

***

Just as they did when George Lanvale blew up part of I-83, news stations interrupted local broadcasts with a special announcement, one that was quickly picked up by the networks and the Internet news services.

"Gunfire erupted on the fifth floor of Baltimore Police Headquarters today, reportedly in the office where the Bright One Task Force was meeting. Police and Federal officials have not yet commented on or confirmed this report, but sources close to this station have informed us that one of the agents suddenly opened fire on the others. We now go live to Police Headquarters where reporter Cathryn Iverson is standing by. Cathryn?"

"Thank you, Jerry. This is Cathryn Iverson live at Police Headquarters where several ambulances arrived just minutes ago. So far police have refused to issue any … wait a minute, something's happening. Yes, we can see several people being wheeled out of the building and into the ambulances. And pulling up now is the Medical Examiner's van. Jerry, that can only indicate that one or more people inside the headquarters building are dead on the scene."

"Thank you, Cathryn. We've just received a statement from the office of Police Commissioner Chester Williams. The statement reads, 'Today there was a shooting incident at a meeting of the Bright One Task Force. It is unknown what prompted this shooting. What is known is that several brave men and women lost their lives. There will be updates as our investigation continues.'"

Pausing for just a moment, the anchorman looked solemn as if mourning the loss of the officers and agents. He then continued.

"While police have refused to disclosed the names of those killed, this station has learned that included among the fallen are BPD detective Bethany Steele, Special Agent Jack Delroy and Agent-in-Charge Charles Guthrie. This station extends its sympathies to their family, friends and co-workers."

In a rented house off Harford Road in northeast Baltimore, as a white-blonde man watched coverage of the tragedy at Police Headquarters one of his associates asked.

"What about that family, Mr. Manion?"

"Forget them, Elson. Mr. Delroy made his choice. We shall abide by it. Call the men in. And prepare to move. It might take them a while, but the police will soon trace our last text to this area. We'd best be gone by then."

***

In the fifth floor conference room of police headquarters, others were watching the coverage as well.

"Looks like they bought it."

Bianca Jones looked at the very much alive Beth Steele and smiled. "Why not? It was on TV, wasn't it?"

She then asked the also still alive Charles Guthrie, "Your men in place?"

"They're ready to move as soon as your 'techno-geeks' find out where that text came from. Or will you be using magic?"

"Haven't you read your Director's memo? There is no such thing as magic."

Bianca looked around the office. Spent shells still littered the floor. There was a hole in the wall caused by the one shot Delroy had been able to get off. It could have gone so wrong …

***

… Jack Delroy had turned pale and, rising, started drawing his service weapon. Beanbags fired from shotguns took him down. Even then he managed to get off a shot, striking nothing but an outside wall. His second shot was interrupted by Greggs who tasered him into submission.

Subdued and back in his chair, Delroy was confronted by a very angry Sergeant Jones.

"Who did they threaten, Delroy. Wife, kids, mother, dog?"

"My girlfriend and her son. They had already killed the dog to prove they could. They said if I told …"

"When?"

"Just before they took the Knox family."

Suddenly Delroy went flying, thrown out of his chair by the small woman in front of him. When he crashed into a corner Bianca was standing over him, staring down, her hand on her gun and maybe hoping that he'd make a sudden move.

Beth Steele and Tavon Greggs backed up their partner, nervously scanning the room watching to see what move the other agents might make. None of them, however, seemed inclined to help Delroy.

"You asshole! You should have told us then."

"But they would have killed …"

"We could have protected them, protected you. You would have been the big hero instead of an accessory to rape, torture and murder."

She turned to Guthrie. "He's one of yours, do what you want with him. Cover it up if you think you have to. Like I said, none of this is gonna end in a trial. Beth, what's on his phone?"

"A text that reads 'Kill them all or the family dies.'"

"Tavon, get that down to Forensics. We need it traced ten minutes ago. And now, to lay a false trail and keep Delroy's family safe, here's what we're going to do …"

***

Triangulation from three towers placed the text as coming from a two block area just south of Harford and Moravia Roads. The plan was to cordon off the area and go house to house if need be and to hell with warrants. Losses were expected, both civilian and law enforcement, but that was a choice with which they'd have to live.

The plan wasn't needed. The feds had their own computer experts, some of whom had been running down home and apartment sales and rentals in the Baltimore area since before the Douglas home was invaded. One of the houses on the list was a block south of Harford and Moravia Roads.

"We isolate the area, then we hit that house," decided Guthrie. "Lieutenant Greggs, can your men contain the perimeter?"

"No one in or out, Sir, except stray dogs. And we'll shoot the dogs if they look suspicious."

Nodding approval, Guthrie turned to Bianca and Beth. "Would you like to join the raiding team?"

"The Freak Show is at your disposal, Sir."

Beth's comment got a dirty look from Bianca and caused Guthrie to redden.

"You're not going to let me forget that, are you, Detective?"

"Not a chance, Sir. Now let's go darken the Bright One's day."

***

The strike force arrived just as two sedans and a mini-van were pulling away from the target house. The feds quickly blocked in and surrounded the vehicles.

The men inside the cars knew what to expect if captured. They been assured by Manion that they were not the only agents of the Bright One. Plea bargains in exchange for their testimony would mean torture and death for their loved ones. If imprisoned they could not be trusted to remain silent forever. One day, one of them would talk. To insure their silence, their families would remain under a sentence of death. If just one man talked, all their loved ones would die.

Best to end things now. To a man they abandoned their cars and rushed to their fate.

The members of the strike force had no problem with that. They had seen what had been done to the Knox family. They had heard how one of their own had been coerced into betrayal. They, too, were willing for things to end on the street rather than in a courtroom.

Twenty trained officers against seven desperate men who had decided to die. The fight was over in a matter of minutes and hail of bullets.

Neither Bianca nor Detective Steele fired a shot or even drew their weapons.

"No sense being placed on admin duty when you don't have to,"

Bianca had pointed out and Beth agreed.

When it was over, Bianca surveyed the results of the legal slaughter. While she had no problem with what had happened, one thing worried her.

"Beth, none of them have white hair."

"Shit!"

The two cops rushed toward the house. Detective Steele's cry of "There's more inside" causing members of the strike force to follow them.

They were on the front porch when Bianca heard a door slam in the rear. Running around to the back, she saw a dark haired man trying to leave. As the sound of gunfire came from inside the man started to draw on her. With little choice, Bianca fired her weapon, striking him twice in the left leg. He fell, dropping his gun.

"You okay?" Beth asked from behind her.

"Yeah, you get him?"

"We got two more, neither of them blonde."

"Damn it!"

Pointing her gun at the fallen man, Bianca asked, "Where's your boss?"

"He left first."

"That's not what I asked."

The captured terrorist shook his head. "There's nothing that you can do to me that he won't do worse to my mother and sister."

"You think not? How about me leaking your name to the media, telling them that thanks to your cooperation we expect to bring down the whole Bright One organization in a matter of weeks?"

The man paled. "You can't. You won't."

Bianca leaned in close, letting the killer see the coldness in her eyes.

"Use your family as bait? You bet your ass I would. What are two lives against all those your boss is going to kill?"

The man moved as if to grab his gun and end things quick.

"Go ahead," he heard, "try it and I'll shoot you so you'll pee sitting down for the rest of your life. And your family will still be bait."

Then he heard his way out.

"Or you can give me what I want and officially you're dead. You'll serve life under a different name and your family will be safe. It's your choice. You've got fifteen seconds."

He gave up a name and address in less than ten.

***

A setback but not an unexpected one, reflected Felix Manion as he calmly packed what he'd need for his flight from Baltimore. Confident in the terror he had instilled in his followers, rather, he corrected himself, the Bright One's followers, he was sure he would have time before this safe house was found.

Soon to be a not so safe house, as the police would no doubt find this one in whatever manner as they had found the last.

He took comfort in knowing that the campaign would go on. A few months, half a year maybe. Let them think it was over. Then people in another city would have to choose between family and innocents. They would be warned as to what was coming, prepared for The Choice they would have to make.

Manion was just about to leave when he heard the sounds outside the house, sounds of cars stopping suddenly. Looking out he saw armed men surrounding the house. Regrettable but again not unexpected. He had known this might happen. One makes his choices and accepts one's fate.

He only hoped that the police would not choose to come in shooting.

***

The raiding party entered to find Felix Manion sitting on a well-used sofa in the living room, his hands in plain view and no weapon in sight.

"A final choice," he told them. "Let me go free or your loved ones die horribly."

"Bullshit!"

Bianca came from behind the armored federal agents and confronted the white-blonde man. "These men were randomly picked an hour before the operation was planned. There is no way you could know them and their names will never be released."

Manion shrugged. "It was worth a try, Sergeant Jones."

At her surprise he continued.

"Oh yes, I know you. Small size, plain features, not much of anything but luck and attitude. Oh yes, I know you, as does the Bright One."

"Never met the man."

"You think not? Let that go for now. But you do have a choice. Take me into custody. Let there be a trial, a trial in which I explain how no one is safe from the choices they make. Especially not the judge, prosecutors, witnesses or the jury members. Especially not their families. They will know this even if it is not said aloud. They will know this from the evidence presented and the way I will look at them. And there's nothing you or anyone else can do to stop that. One or more will choose the safe road and hold out for acquittal. Each and every time I'm tried."

"You mentioned a choice."

"So I did, Sergeant. You can kill me now."

Bianca's voice was calm and steady as she said, "Everybody out."

She expected someone to protest. No one did. They all knew that this was a choice to be made by one person and acted on with no witnesses present.

"You heard the lady, everybody get out."

"You too, Beth." Bianca's voice was now cold as ice.

"Your choice, Miss Jones," Manion said once they were alone.

"You really only have one choice, Miss Jones. We both know what it is. It's an easy decision. It's in your job description. You hunt monsters. You kill them with no questions asked. And am I not as much of a monster than any you've met?

"Listen to them out there, shuffling their feet, waiting for you to pull the trigger. They want you to do it. By now one them has probably has the gun they'll 'find' on my body, the gun I was going for when you 'had' to kill me."

Manion's face, his voice were those of a man who knew he was making sense, that he was echoing the thoughts of his listener.

"So easy, Miss Jones, when you consider the alternative. Mistrial after mistrial, each one followed by people dying horribly. Sooner or later, someone will make the choice that you should make today."

Bianca knew that Manion was right. It would be easy, she thought. So easy to take out my gun and kill, no, execute him. That's what they want. That's what he wants, the choice he wants me to make. The easy choice, to call a man a monster and pull the trigger. And the next time, and the times after that it would be easier still until my soul withers away.

But if I let this – man – live, people will die, innocent people who could have been saved with a single bullet. And each death will haunt my dreams.

As if sensing her thought, Manion smiled. "Damned if you do, damned if you don't. Each must choose their own damnation."

Must I, Bianca thought, then to Manion, "Must I? What if I choose not to be damned?"

"You haven't been paying attention, Miss Jones. That's never been an option."

It was the detective's turn to smile as she made her decision. "It is now. Manion, it's time for you to die."

Bianca raised her gun and Manion went down.

***

Slowly, painfully, Felix Manion returned to consciousness. He was lying down, a bandage seemingly wrapped around his head. He tried to feel it but both his hands were tied to his bed. When his eyes came back into focus, he saw two uniformed men with nasty looking weapons standing between his bed and a door, one facing out, one facing him.

Sensing the presence of someone else Manion turned. A woman was standing at the foot, a small woman.

"You're in the hospital wing of a federal prison in … well, you don't need to know that," came the voice of Bianca Jones "You've been out for a day and half. Mostly sedatives, I didn't hit you that hard."

"You really should have killed me, Miss Jones."

"You wanted me to, wanted to bring me down to your level. To be damned as much as you are. And to do that you were willing to martyr yourself for the Bright One, whatever he is."

"You'll find out soon enough."

"No doubt. But as for my not killing you, who says I didn't."

Picking up a remote, Bianca turned the TV to the news channel.

"If you watch long enough, you'll see yourself, or rather, a very good computer simulation. You'll be in a police interrogation room. There you'll turn against your master. Weeping uncontrollably, you'll renounce all that the Bright One made you do and express deep remorse for your actions. Then sometime tonight in a fit of despair you'll hang yourself with your own somewhat soiled underwear."

"You can't do this."

"We can, we have. Tomorrow, after you're 'dead' you'll be transferred to a Philadelphia prison under a new name. There you'll start serving a life sentence in solitary for killing two federal agents. It seems that there's a messy murder/suicide the government wants to cover up."

"Whatever you do to me won't stop the Bright One from coming."

"If he does, we'll be ready for him. I'll be ready for him. Remember what you said? I hunt monsters. I kill them. If the Bright One wants to come, well, that's his choice."

MAN ON THE INSIDE

They came in the early morning. DeWitt Jackson heard the pounding at the door, the tearing of the hinges, and the breaking of the wood but there was nothing he could do. No 9-1-1, the phone was out. No chance to get his piece. That was locked up because of the kids. He prayed it was just a burglary and feared it wasn't.

He turned, wanting to wake his wife, wanting to tell her to get under the bed or in the bathroom, someplace she wouldn't be seen right away. Her side was cold and empty.

She's downstairs, he realized. She did that when she couldn't sleep. That meant …

They were in his bedroom before he could rush to her side. There were two of them – Clay and Little Auds.

Their guns were out, their faces unmasked. That could only mean one thing.

"Cop." From Clay's mouth it was a death sentence.

"You don't want to do this," Jackson argued uselessly.

Little Auds smiled. "We sure as shit do."

Sound of a struggle and a woman's cry came from downstairs. "My wife."

"Will be taken care of," Clay said coldly, "by all of us. Always wanted to do a cop's wife, do her the way you did us."

Keep them talking, play for time; maybe the neighbors heard something, called it in.

Noises came from the other bedroom.

"My boys."

"Too bad for them their daddy was a snitch cop."

"They're not part of this, Clay. They're innocents."

"Then they'll go right to heaven, won't they. Go take care of them, Auds."

"Sure thing, Clay."

Little Auds left the room and Jackson made his move, hoping to catch Clay off guard. Instead the man's pistol smashed into his face, knocking him to the floor.

"For that you die slow." Clay grabbed a pillow, fired through it. Two into the gut, another into the groin.

"Your wife will die slower, when we're done with her. As for your kids …" Two muffled shots came from the rear bedroom, "They'll be waiting for their daddy, if you are their daddy and their momma didn't whore around like she's gonna do all this week."

Jackson did not hear Clay leave or the man's final words. He had blacked out, only to have the pain bring him back. Fight it, he told himself, stay with it. Why, came the answer from inside. Too late to save Alexia, too late for the kids. Not too late to make them pay. Stay with it, someone will come, they have to pay. I'll make them all pay if it's the last thing I do. Just hold on, someone will come …

No one did, not until later that morning, when a neighbor on his way to work saw the kitchen door standing open. By then it was too late for DeWitt Jackson.

***

Frank's Hall was a cop bar just off Harford Road on 25th Street. It was usually a place for good times and celebration but a week after Jackson's murder it was the scene of a wake for a fallen comrade.

"What have you got on it," Sergeant Bianca Jones asked of her friend and sometime partner Bethany Steele.

The homicide detective shook her head. "We got prints and DNA that belong to the victims, we got cartridge cases and bullets but no guns to match them to and we got no witnesses. In short, Bianca, we got squat."

"I thought there were suspects, the gang he was into."

"All of whom swear that that they were in Atlantic City for the weekend. Cell phone records and receipts from hotel rooms and ATMs back them up."

"Those are easy enough to fake, Beth."

"And damn hard to refute, at least in front of a Baltimore jury that hates cops as much as it does snitches. These Southwest Boys are monsters, and they might walk. They're going to walk unless we get something, anything."

Bianca shook her head. "Sorry, Beth, not my kind of monsters. Show me a supernatural or occult connection and I'll shut them down and send them to Hell. But until you do … besides, Williams has me working on the kiddie porn case that that freak Patton handed us."

"Just asking. We all want to get these guys, Bianca. It's not good to let scum like this get away with killing cops."

***

In the southwest corner of Baltimore, just off Wetheredsville Road and north of Leakin Park there is a vacant lot on which there is sometimes a house. The house disappeared one rainy winter's night and for weeks after those who lived nearby swore that they could hear the screams of those who were inside when it vanished. When it returned a few months later the bodies that were found inside were not of those who were in the house when it disappeared.

A month after this the house vanished again. When it reappeared the city ordered that it be torn down. This was quickly done by workers paid three times the going rate. The day after it was razed, the rubble that had been left behind was gone. Two days after the murder of Officer Jackson the house came back.

***

It hurts, was the first thing DeWitt Jackson thought as he returned to consciousness. Then, it was just a dream, a horrible dream as the pain slowly faded away. A dream? Then what are you doing on the floor?

Jackson stood and looked around. The bed was unmade. There was blood where he had fallen. Black powder was on his bedroom door.

Crime scene, his cop senses told him. My crime scene. Walking over to the door he tried to close it so as to look at himself in the full length mirror hung on its back but his hand could not grasp the knob. Not thinking, he turned to the dresser mirror to see if there were holes in his tee shirt and sleep pants. He did not see the holes, nor did he see himself.

Glancing down, he saw two holes in his black shirt and one in his grey pants. Looking up he again failed to appear in the mirror.

Slowly his new reality became clear to him. Even as he struggled to accept it he walked to his boys' room. The door was closed. Unable to turn the knob he still somehow passed through the door.

He saw that the pillows were gone and that the beds were cut open from the lab techs' search for bullets. There was no blood.

One more thing. Downstairs he found the living room as it should be – no blood, nothing disturbed, no sign of his wife. "Alexia, I'm sorry," he said, hoping his wife was now some place where she could hear him.

It was only then that Jackson allowed himself to put the pieces together. I was killed but here I am. I can't grab things but I can walk through doors. I can't see myself in a mirror. He then remembered his thoughts before the blackness took him. "I'll make them pay if it's the last thing I do."

Ghost, he thought. Looks like I have some haunting to do.

Jackson moved toward the front door. It was closed and as he expected, his hand could not grasp the knob. Not a problem he thought and tried to pass through the door. He could not. Nor could he exit through the kitchen door or any of the walls or windows. Trapped in the house where he and his family had been destroyed Jackson gave way to despair, no one hearing his moans of anguish though they lasted through the night.

On the days following, Jackson wandered the home that had become his prison, trying to remember the good times his family had had in it, but always going back to the rooms where he was murdered and his family killed or taken. "What Ifs" filled his thoughts – what if I hadn't become a cop, what if I hadn't transferred into Narcotics, what if I hadn't volunteered to go under – and he searched his mind trying to figure out where, when and how his cover had been blown.

On the fourth day after he was gunned down, his front door opened. Sunni, a detective he knew from the force, came in. He led in what looked like a cleaning crew.

"We're done with the house, so you guys can have it now," he told them. "To tell you the truth, we were done the next day but the State's Attorney wanted it held for some reason known only to her."

"Sunni!" Jackson shouted but the detective did not hear him. "Sunni," he yelled again, then realized that if he could not be seen it was likely that he could not be heard. Still he tried again. Going up the man, he stood next to him and shouted as loud as he could but still there was no reaction.

"It was worth a try," Jackson said to the unhearing Sunni, "But hey, maybe when you leave I can go out the door with you." Not thinking, he put his hand on the detective's shoulder. As the hand passed through his body Sunni shivered.

"You okay?" asked one of the crime scene cleanup crew.

"A cold chill just passed through me, that's all."

"Yeah, I get them from time to time. Listen, unless you have to, you don't got to hang around. We'll lock up when we're done and get the keys to the sister."

"Thanks." The detective opened the door to leave, Jackson right beside him. But as Sunni left, some force held Jackson back.

"Damn it," Jackson cried out, the open door an invisible barrier he alone could not cross. As he stood in the doorway looking at the world seemingly denied him, one of the cleanup crew needing equipment passed through him. As the crewman shivered, Jackson felt a tug towards the outside.

Maybe I can't leave on my own, he thought, but maybe I can hitch a ride.

Jackson waited and watched the crew wash away the signs of his murder. When they finished, he matched the pace of the first to leave and as that man crossed the threshold so did Jackson.

Expecting to be thrown back into his house, Jackson was pleased and surprised to find himself on the outside. *Thanks*, he thought to his unwitting rescuer.

"You're welcome," was the unexpected reply.

Even as the man wondered who had thanked him and why, Jackson realized that he man had heard him. This discovery, along with his new found freedom, gave him some hope that he might accomplish the task he had ahead of him.

***

It was good in the old garage that the Southwest Boys used as their headquarters. Parrot and his crew had brought in the cash from the street and it was enough that Clay had given word that weed and rock was free for the night. Dreds brought in some girls to make it a proper party.

On a chair against the east wall, a nice piece called Deanna on his lap, Little Auds had one hand up her shirt and the other sliding around her butt when a sudden chill took him. Auds stood and, dropping Deanna to the floor, shook like he had the flu.

The girl's scream got everyone looking. Clay nodded to a couple of the boys. "Take him to the office – and shut that bitch up." A slap took care of Deanna while Auds was dragged to the back.

Lying on a dirty cot in what had once been the business office, Little Auds was feeling better. The shaking had stopped. He had just started wondering what had been in the weed he'd smoked when the chills came over him again. This time, however, there was a voice.

Little Auds, it said, *aka Desmond Brian Woods.*

Auds shook his head to clear it. That was some bad weed. Or maybe it was the forty he had drank before.

It's neither one, Woods, came the answer to his thoughts. *What it is, is payback time.*

He didn't want to, but Little Auds got off the cot. Against his will he walked to the desk where he knew that Clay kept a clean 9mm. On their own his hands took out the pistol, checked its load and racked one into the chamber.

Do you know, Woods, it's a damn long walk from the northeast to here. As the voice spoke to him Auds's legs moved him toward the party in the front room. *Even if you don't get tired, or hungry, or sleepy, it's a damn long walk, especially if all you can do is think about what you lost, what was taken from you. But there were things to do, like practice on strangers. Practice making them hear you, practice making them turn right instead of left. Practice making them do what you say, go where you want.*

Auds was close to the office door. The voice kept talking in his head. *I got good at it, Woods. Very good. Too bad for you and your friends.*

His hand was turning the knob when, Auds found his voice. "Just who the hell are you?"

No answer. Auds would have thought it a drug dream but then he was through the door, raising the nine, squeezing the trigger, emptying the clip.

Clay was the first to drop, then Dreds. More fell after that, those that didn't find cover. Parrot, his own piece in his hand, fired back. Deanna and two other girls caught stray rounds as others joined in, shooting at Auds, at shadows, at anything that moved.

A target in the doorway, Auds could make no move to avoid the bullets that came his way. He was struck once, twice, four then five times. When his body was finally allowed to collapse, the voice was still with him, laughing inside his head as if enjoying his pain.

Sirens in the distance. The cops would be there soon. This one will be on me, Auds thought. He knew that if anyone was left alive they'd give him up to avoid the charge themselves. And the hell of it was he didn't do it, didn't mean to anyway.

"Why?" he asked the thing inside him.

You should have asked why before you killed me and took my family, was the answer.

An image in his mind, him and Clay killing a rat cop. Then Auds knew.

"But we didn't …"

Then all was gone except the sound of laughter.

Standing amidst the dead, dying and wounded, Jackson waited, expecting something to happen. Just what he didn't know. For judgment maybe. For the Gates of Heaven to open for him. The Flames of Hell to consume him. Maybe just a slow fade into oblivion. But something should happen now that Clay was dead and Little Auds ready to follow him. Most of the other Southwest Boys were gone as well. The gang was broken. Jackson's job was done.

So why am I still here?

The police and medics arrived. Bodies dead and otherwise were carried out. Detectives came and asked questions. Lab guys came and took pictures. With nothing else to do and nowhere to go Jackson stayed to watch, still asking himself,

Why am I still here? Maybe, he thought, it's because I'm still a cop and this is where I should be, on a scene, on the street, where I'm comfortable. I guess old habits die hard and continue after death.

It was only after everyone else had gone and he was alone in the dark that Jackson again recalled his last living thoughts.

I'll make them all pay if it's the last thing I do.

All pay.

All.

There were gangs other than the Southwest Boys, gangs that ran whores, sold dope and dealt death. All of them were somehow responsible for his death and what had happened to his family. They would all pay.

***

Beth Steele was working on surviving victim reports from Sinai and St. Agnes Hospitals when voices came over her cubicle wall.

"It's the craziest thing," said Detective Donal McLarney.

"What?" replied Sunni, "that one drug-crazed gangboy goes nuts and kills a bunch of people? That's not crazy, that's Baltimore, bunk."

"It's not that," McLarney replied. "I took his statement down at Shock Trauma. You know what he said about why he did it?"

In her mind Beth pictured Sunni shrugging as he said, "Because someone took the last joint?"

"No, he said it was because the ghost of DeWitt Jackson was haunting him, all but admitted to his murder."

"We always figured the Boys had done it, now we know. A kind of justice for Jackson. Doped up and a guilty conscience, a bad combination."

So intently was Beth listening to the detectives' conversation that she didn't hear Major Pompey Fredericks come up behind her. It wasn't until the commander of the Homicide Unit cleared her throat that Beth knew was there.

She moves quiet for such a large woman, the detective thought.

"I heard the same thing you did, Steele," the Major said. "You heard the word ghost and right now you're thinking that maybe you should call your buddy Jones over in Special Ops. I know that you and she have worked some weird shit together, just as I know that vampires, demons and werewolves are real. But this, whatever it is and whatever it turns into, stays in house. This is our case and one that the Freak Show gets no part of. Understood?"

"Yes, Major." Then Beth dared to add, "Bianca Jones has her own ways of finding things out."

"I know, and one day she'll find out too much. But not this time. Desmond Woods's confession closed this case and Officer Jackson's murder. Let the dead rest in peace, Detective."

***

Desmond Woods died in the hospital, but not of his wounds. Two nights after he was admitted, with an officer outside his room standing guard, Woods pulled out the IVs that were keeping him alive. It was believed that he had done this in his sleep. No one suspected a spectral presence that tormented him for twenty minutes before finally forcing him to take his own life.

That same night, two gangbangers just hanging at Walbrook Junction were gunned down by a shooter who simply walked up to them and opened fire. The first rounds dropped them, the next several were fired as the gunman stood over them and emptied his clip. When the police arrived he told them a story about being forced to do it.

The shooter was identified as Ivan Perez, a low-level gofer for the Gwynn Oak Ninjas, an offshoot of the Clifton Park Crewe. After being booked, Perez was beaten to death by a Walbrook pusher who felt it his duty to represent the Junction. When news of Perez's murder got out, it took four days before the retaliatory shootings stopped.

Five dead, four seriously wounded, two paralyzed for life and one blinded. Most were gang members or drug dealers. One was a fourteen year old girl who would never dance, drive a car, or ever get out of her wheelchair. The other was a young boy who would have been ten had he lived.

It was not enough. DeWitt Jackson still walked unseen through the streets of Baltimore wondering how many more it would take.

The kid, the girl, they weren't my fault, he told himself. The gangs did that. More would have to die. All of them would pay.

Working twelve hour shifts with all leaves cancelled, Homicide and district detectives identified suspects and made arrests. One of those arrested was Leandro Shepard who just two weeks before had been found not guilty of a brutal double murder. His lawyer, Mitchell Raleigh, had won the acquittal by attacking the off duty behavior of the primary investigator, convincing the jury that the detective's affair with his wife's sister somehow tainted DNA, fingerprint, and witness identifications.

News of Shepard's new arrest and the circumstances of his release prompted outrage in official circles, editorials in the press, and an increase in clients for Raleigh and Associates. It also attracted the attention of DeWitt Jackson, who had stopped in a tavern to watch the news on the always-on television.

Damn lawyers, he thought, suddenly realizing who his next target should be.

Raleigh's death went viral. His office was wired for sound and video, a needed precaution he had installed given the kind of people he represented, lawyer/client privilege be damned. The video of his death was released by his partner and lover who did not want the world to think that the most special person in his life had committed suicide.

On the video Raleigh is alone in his office. He shivers, then stiffens. He tries to move but cannot. What words he speaks come hard.

"What ... who ... but you're dead ... the Southwest Boys ... The Walbrook murder ... you? They weren't my clients ... It's my job ... it's my duty ... they're not guilty, not until a jury says so ... No, I won't ... you can't make ..."

Seemingly struggling against his own body, Raleigh opens his desk drawer and takes out a .38 special, another precaution against dissatisfied clients. Slowly he puts the gun in his mouth, his body fighting itself all the time. With his arm stiff and his hand shaking, his finger tightens on the trigger. A loud pop, his head goes back and his arm falls, dropping the revolver. His body lies lifeless until the video cuts off.

Drugs were blamed. So were CIA mind control and radio waves

from Venus. When a popular cable show blamed ghosts a trauma nurse who had attended Desmond Woods remembered him blaming fallen police officer DeWitt Jackson for his slaughter of the Southwest Boys. A prisoner who had shared a cell with Ivan Perez recalled that Perez had claimed that a voice in his head had forced him to commit murder.

In a south Baltimore tavern, former Officer Jackson stood and wondered when his time on Earth would be over. With nothing else to do, he watched television and waited for the news to tell him who else had to die.

****

Beth Steele would have given a week's pay to have listened in on the meeting between Major Fredericks and Bianca Jones. Bianca had fought vampires, monsters, fire demons and the devil himself, but it took a special kind of courage to face down Pompey Fredericks on her own turf. Whatever was said, the two women did not part as friends.

"This will not be forgotten, Sergeant," came the major's voice as Bianca left her office.

"Good," Bianca replied, "that way, Major, you'll always remember a girl in a wheelchair and a mother who buried her son."

On her way out of the Homicide Unit, Bianca stopped at Beth's cubicle. "You should have said something." Her voice was flat, leaving the detective to read into what she would – disappointment, a sense of betrayal, a kind of reprimand. Bianca left before Beth could reply.

Once off duty, Beth stopped at Morgan's Books, an alley shop in Baltimore's historic Fells Point. The shop was owned by Bianca's husband Joe and it was much more than a bookstore, just as Joe Russo was much more than a book seller. Every time Beth entered it she marveled at how its interior seemed so much larger the than its exterior.

Joe looked up from the front counter as the detective entered. "She's in the back," he said. Beth found Bianca staring at Joe's collection of occult books.

"I thought Joe was the only one those things talked to."

Without looking her way, Bianca said, "Five thousand years of mystical and magical knowledge. Forbidden lore from more than a dozen worlds. Demons fought over some of these books. Angels killed over some of these books. Scholars gave their lives, some lost their souls to acquire them. Pick one off the shelf. If you could read it, it might show you how to rule the world or destroy it. And yet not one of the damned things could tell Joe how to find a ghost at large in my city."

"Nothing on ghosts and spirits?"

"Plenty. Joe says that there are books that tell you how to banish a ghost from a house, how to trap one in a spirit bottle, even how to exorcise one from a Porter touring car, but there's nothing on how to find a vengeful dead cop wandering the city killing people."

"Joe can't track him with that similarity spell of his?" Beth asked. "It's worked before."

"Using our perp's DNA. But that would only lead us to Jackson's dead body. I know where that is, I had it dug up last night."

"Why?"

"I was hoping that our favorite medical examiner could do that voodoo he does so well and draw Jackson's soul back into its body, but Dominic said that the autopsy had ruined the body for that trick."

"It might not be DeWitt's ghost. It could just be …"

"Right, it could just be a set of bizarre coincidences. I hope to God it is. But it's my job to act as if it's not, to think zebras instead of horses."

The two women were silent for a while, the only noises coming from the front as Joe closed up the shop.

"How can I help?" Beth finally asked.

"Pull the case files, all the murders starting from Jackson's plus his undercover work. Look for something, anything that doesn't look right. And stay out of Fredericks's way."

Beth shrugged off the warning. "She'll yell and scream but that's about all. I clear too many murders for her to do anything else. And Bianca, about not telling you …"

"Forget it, I shouldn't have blamed you. Until Raleigh died there was nothing to tell. And now …If the only victims were the gangers and the dealers, I could live with that. Those people deal death and should be paid in their own coin."

"I know, Bianca, the women in the garage, the kid, the girl, even that lawyer, none of them deserved …"

"I wasn't thinking of them, Beth. I was thinking of Jackson himself. I want to find him before he's lost forever."

***

Later, when Bianca and Joe were alone in the shop …

"You're sure that none of these books can tell you how to find a ghost?"

"They don't tell me a thing, Bianca. But somehow I'm aware of what's in each one of them. Many of them tell how to find ghosts, but in a city like Baltimore, or any big city, with all the pain, suffering and violent death, there can be so many ghosts that there's no way in the world to find a particular one."

"Well, if we can't find Jackson, why not have him come to us? The Commissioner could form a special task force to look into these deaths, announce that I'm in charge of it. Jackson was a cop, he'd know what that would mean."

"That the Freak Show was after him."

"You know I hate that name."

"Doesn't mean you're not stuck with it."

"Doesn't mean you have to use it. But you're right. Knowing my group was after him might force him to come after me the way he did Raleigh."

"And when he takes you over?"

"I can handle him. I've done it before."

"The monster in your dream house, the one that wound up trapped inside you?" At Bianca's nod Joe went on. "A couple of problems with that. Assuming you could 'handle' him, what are you going to do then? Walk around with the spirit of an angry dead cop in your head? Dump him in Hell like you did the monster? And what if you can't 'handle' him and he kills you like he did Raleigh?"

"Death's always a risk for a cop, Joe."

"So what if he uses your body to kill others? Beth, Tavon, me? Or if he uses one of us to kill you? As plans go this was not one of your better ones."

After listening to her husband, Bianca was quiet, angry quiet. She hated being wrong, hated the fact that her being wrong could have led to the deaths of those she loved and cared for. It was her job to stop Jackson and she had no idea how to find him. Joe had said it, there was no way in the world ...

"No way in this world," Bianca said out loud. "So what about another one?" She told him the idea that had come to her.

"It's still risky ... I know, everything you do is, but this one ... Jackson's killed a lot of people. Whether he knows it or not, he's absorbed some of their life's energies. He gets stronger with each death."

"I've killed people myself, Joe. I've killed things that are more than people. I think, no, I sure I'm stronger that he is. Tomorrow I'll review the reports from Beth. Tomorrow night this ends."

***

In her office the next morning, Bianca reviewed case files, starting with Raleigh's murder and working backwards to Jackson's.

Has anyone told her? she wondered. She's no doubt heard the speculation on the news, maybe seen the video, but has anyone talked to her? No matter. If this thing gets resolved tonight and I'm still here tomorrow I'll deal with it then.

Later that night, in her apartment …

"That's what you're wearing to bed?" Joe asked seeing Bianca in what she called her work clothes – sweater, jeans and a windbreaker jacket to hide her weapon. A department shield was pinned to the front of the jacket.

"What would you like me to wear to bed," she asked, knowing the answer.

"Nothing."

"Whatever I wear to bed is what I wear in my dreams. And I don't want to confront Jackson naked. Tomorrow night I'll wear, or not wear, whatever you like."

"Are you sure this is going to work?"

"Let's hope so. Poe called sleep a little slice of death. Holding to that belief should help in finding the plane that Jackson's on. That, and this."

Bianca pointed to the badge.

"That's not yours."

"No, it's Jackson's. I got it out of Evidence Control. It should help me focus on him."

"And when you find him?"

"Then it's up to him – he goes down easy, he goes down hard, or he goes away. Let's do this."

Bianca lies on her bed in a mostly darkened room, Joe watching her from a chair in the corner. On the table next to him was a pistol. "In case something comes back in my body," Bianca had told him. Despite ten years in the Baltimore Police Crime Lab Joe had never fired a gun in his life. He hoped that he wouldn't have to that night and prayed that he would have the courage to do so if their worst fears came true.

Bianca laid on her bed, her eyes closed, the words from a childhood game, the words she uses to enter her dream house, running through her mind.

You are standing in front of a large mansion. Slowly, the front door opens. You step inside. In front of you is a long flight of stairs. You ascend ...

Slowly, Bianca dropped off to sleep. When she seemingly awoke she was in a long hallway, ten doors on either side with one at the end of the passage. That was the room of red and black, the room of death. She had entered it only once and left with a monster inside her.

Idly she wondered if the house in the Southwest that was sometimes there and sometimes not was someone else's dream house. Could she, from hers, get inside it and if so, what she would discover behind its door? But one problem at a time. She had a killer to find.

Sleep is a slice of death, she told herself. Concentrating on Jackson, she let his badge guide her steps.

Noises came from behind the doors – sighs of passion, screams of pain, shouts of joy, cries of despair. There were times when she would have investigated these sounds but tonight was a night to leave them be. She walked until midway down she felt a tug toward one door. Behind it she heard laughter, arguing, the clink of glasses and the noise of a TV. She opened it and found herself in a bar.

She knew the place, had been there for retirements, weddings and wakes. It was the 10-44, a cop bar in the Southern District. A game was on and the off duty men and women of the Southern and Southwest police districts were halfway watching it and half talking about their shifts and complaining about their jobs.

No one noticed her. They wouldn't, she was not of their world. For tonight at least I'm dead to them. Looking around, she saw someone else who was as well.

Jackson was leaning against the wall in a pose Bianca knew well from high school. Always on the edge of the crowd, wanting to be noticed by the popular ones, never called on and never asked to join in. All one could do was watch others have fun.

Life as a ghost. Or maybe this is Jackson's Hell or Purgatory. Where does he go when the bars close? What does he do? Does he go home with any of these? Does he go home as one of these, stealing a little joy out of their lives?

Jackson had yet to notice her. Looking past his bloodstained shirt and pants she looked for and found his spirit self – mostly grey, too much black, only a little of the brightness of his soul shining through.

Bianca dared to look at her own self in the mirror behind the bar. No black, more grey than she would like, more brightness than she thought.

Jackson was now staring in her direction. Time to get this done, she thought.

What the … It was the light reflected from the mirror that drew his attention. The light that was coming from the short chick coming toward him. Did she, could she see him? He knew her, had heard of her. Her name was Jones and she headed a squad that people had started calling the Freak Show. They said she hunted monsters and things that were not quite real. But that would mean …

"Good evening, Officer Jackson. You and I have a lot to talk about."

She was there to stop him, stop him from doing what he must to find peace, stop him from taking down all those responsible for his family. He went for her, not knowing what might happen when ghost met spirit.

He did not expect to find himself flying across the room, his body passing through the bar's patrons who took no notice of his passage.

Okay, he thought. New situation, old rules. Jackson looked at his opponent. No problem there. He was close to six feet, she was maybe five-one. He had weight on him, she was barely there. He was a cop, used to the brutality of the street, she was some kind of detective, one who showed up after the rough and tumble was over. This would be easy.

DeWitt Jackson may have heard of Bianca Jones but he didn't know her. He didn't know that she had faced people like him all her life, people who saw only her size, people who constantly underestimated her.

She let him come. When he got close enough a kick to his knee and a knee to his groin dropped him hard. He came back up, punched her in the face. Staggered but not down, Bianca ducked another blow then hit his armpit hard.

Jackson's right side went dead but his opponent was close enough to grab and this time it was Bianca who sailed across the room.

Damn, she thought, this is going to take longer than I thought. Then she realized that it could go even longer than that. They were both spirits, short of death neither could inflict any lasting harm on the other. Time for a change of scene.

She rushed him, stopping short just as he reached for her. Bianca grabbed and, using his body against him, threw him through the wall, concentrating as she did.

What in the hell? Jackson looked around. He was on a city street, one he knew, Jefferson and Lakewood.

"Remember this place?" The voice of Detective Jones came from behind him. He turned, ready to resume their conflict.

"It's your first post, DeWitt, back when you were a cop, back when this meant something to you."

Something metal hit the pavement in front of him. Looking down, Jackson saw that it was a badge, his badge. He let it lay.

"That was before."

"Before what, DeWitt? Before you chose murder over justice, before you decided that innocent lives didn't matter."

"I didn't shoot those people."

Bianca knew who he meant – the women in the club, the ten year old, the girl in the wheelchair. "You started it. You caused it. It's on you."

Jackson squared, ready to fight again. "Don't matter. I'll do what I have to."

"Why?"

"Like I said, don't matter. Let's go, I got nothing else to do."

"But I do." Drawing her pistol, Bianca shot him, first in the shoulder, then in the thigh, avoiding killing shots. Jackson fell. Bianca stood over him.

"Don't get up," she warned, "or the next one goes in your head and you'll find out what happens to a ghost when he dies."

"You bitch, you shot me!"

"And I'll shoot you again if you don't start listening and answering questions. Now what do you have to do and why?"

The pain was real, and as bad as the night he was killed. But already Jackson felt it lessening. There was, however, the short, crazy lady ready to make it hurt again.

"I want to move on but I can't. I made a promise. To get them if it's the last thing I did. But I'm still here. So whatever I've done, it's not enough. Somewhere, the ones responsible are still out there. I just don't know who."

"Clay Brown and Little Auds are dead."

"I know, I killed them, like they killed me, like they killed my boys. But Auds, he wouldn't tell me about my wife, what they did with her. Said he didn't know about that. Said he didn't know who dimed me out."

"You wife is fine, DeWitt. She's with her sister. Your boys are with her."

"Bullshit, I heard them die. I heard the shots. And Clay said …"

"Clay was lying, drug dealing scum and a cruel son of a bitch. You got close enough to know that. He'd say anything to torture your last minutes."

"But Alexia, we put the boys to bed together, we went to sleep together. And I heard the shots, saw their bed."

"We didn't find your boys, just a shot up bed. Your wife ... she told us that you two had a big fight, that she spent the night at her sister's."

"Then she … lied."

The truth rushed in and with it a pain that was worse than any before. "She …lied."

"Did she know," Bianca asked gently, "about your undercover?"

The pain from the bullets had faded. His eyes on Bianca, making no sudden moves, Jackson slowly stood up.

"Not the where and who, just that I was on assignment."

"Who did, on our end?"

"The guys on the squad, the sarge and the lieutenant."

Her reading of follow up reports now told Bianca the rest of the story. She led Jackson to it. "Who asked you to do the job?"

"The Sarge, Josh McCall, why?"

"Since your murder, he's been to see your wife, several times."

First his wife, then a friend. The pain of betrayal got worse. But at least now Jackson saw an end to it.

"Thank you very much, Detective Jones. Tell your bosses two more and it will all be over."

"I can't let you leave, DeWitt."

"You can't stop me and you can't hide them away. Not forever. I've got nothing but time. I'll find them, then I'll find peace."

"There's no peace in Hell, DeWitt, just despair and misery. And that's where you're headed. I've seen your soul, it's black with sin. But there's some goodness left in you. Stop now and you've a chance at redemption. Otherwise all hope is lost."

"I'll take that chance."

"I won't let you." Bianca raised her pistol.

"Go ahead, shoot. Put me down and tap me twice. I'll take my hate to Hell and you'll have put me there. If you can kill me. Somehow I don't think this death will take either."

"Your boys lost their father. You'd take their mother from them, make them orphans?"

"What other choice do I have?"

Bianca thought for a moment, then told him.

* * *

Two nights later, Josh McCall was on a stakeout down in O'Donnell Heights. He wasn't looking for dealers or runners. His drug unit knew where there were. He was watching the cars that stopped and the people who got out. He took their pictures and copied their tags. Later these people would get a visit from a Drug Enforcement detective and would be threatened with arrest if they were ever caught buying drugs in the city again.

Fat lot of good it'll do, McCall said to himself. Damn judges'll just give them probation before judgment and a fine. Thinking about "damn judges" led to McCall thinking about damn lawyers and from there to what happened to Mitchell Raleigh and how that was somehow DeWitt Jackson's fault.

This ghost business is bullshit, McCall decided. Damn shame about Jackson, but what you gonna do? Jackson's fine wife was willing to share but I wasn't. And the SWB paid nice for the info on him. Getting harder and harder to get by on cop pay even with the OT.

A pick-up drove past McCall and parked. A guy and girl got out, late teens by the looks of them. Pennsylvania plates again, third one tonight. They think it's fun to come down to the big, bad city to buy drugs. Let's see how much fun it is when …

That's when the headache hit him. A blinding pain that robbed him of his vision and seemed like daggers in his skull. It lasted only a few minutes but left McCall wasted and near collapse.

Just as it was over, just as McCall was thinking stroke or brain cancer it got worse.

Did you like that, Sarge? asked a voice inside his head. As the voice went on, McCall realized that ghosts weren't bullshit.

You did for me and you're doing my wife. You left me with nothing, less than nothing so now it's payback time.

Another headache, more blindness and pain.

I killed those people, just like they said. Now it's your turn. But you're not going to die, not for what you did.

Headache. Blindness. Pain.

Get used to it. Every day, every hour. Maybe twice, three times an hour. For the rest of your life.

A whispered "Please" was followed by "We can work some ..."

Work something out? There's nothing I want, no where you can go. Well, maybe there's one thing I want, and one place you can go.

Headache. Blindness. Pain.

***

Bianca Jones was with Alexia Jackson when the news broke that BPD Sergeant Josh McCall had confessed to exposing DeWitt's undercover to the Southwest Boys.

"What did your boys see?"

Alexia shook her head. "Nothing, I got them out of the house right after ... the break in."

"McCall won't mention your name, or how you betrayed DeWitt," the detective told the woman. "You're safe as long as you raise the boys right."

Alexia looked at Bianca, not wanting to but somehow believing all that she had been told about the aftermath of her husband's death, a death in which she had a part.

"And if I don't?"

"There's no statute of limitation on felonies in Maryland. I can and will put you away whenever I feel like it. Besides, DeWitt will be watching you."

Somewhere in Alexia's mind came her husband's voice, *You can bet your ass on that.*

Shivering with a chill not caused by any cold, she looked around. Seeing no one, Alexia turned toward Bianca but the detective had already left.

***

The next night, dressed in her "work clothes," Bianca again sought her dream house. This time she went straight to the door that opened into the 10-44. Seeing Jackson leaning against a wall, she motioned him over to an empty table. When he sat she handed him a beer.

"How did you ..."

"I'm dreaming, I can do anything."

"And I'm still a ghost, I haven't moved on."

"You got sins to pay for. Sparing McCall and forgiving Alexia was a start, but just a start."

"So what am I supposed to do? I can't hang around in bars all my afterlife."

"You could work for me."

"Join the Freak Show?" Jackson thought about it for a moment then shrugged. "What do you need me to do, Chief?"

"There's a house in the Southwest that's only sometimes there. I could use a man on the inside."

WHOEVER FIGHTS GODS

"Coffee?" asked the being in absolute black. The one in brilliant white nodded his agreement. The two sat at a table on the outskirts of Hell as uncommitted souls wailed their despair around them.

"Are you quite certain about this course of action, Apollonius?"

"More than ever, Morningstar."

"Then I suggest you try someplace other than the Charmed City."

"Just because you failed there doesn't mean I will. Besides, I have a debt to pay."

Satan smiled. "The debt you tried to collect in Gotham?"

The Bright One shrugged. "A miscalculation. Her first. Then him, or rather what's left of him."

"Well, if you'll take my advice ..."

"Why should I? Consider where your judgment has brought you?"

"Then learn from my misfortune. She's beaten you twice. Your plan to corrupt her failed and before that ... which did she do? Impale or decapitate you? You must be tired of edged weapons by now. By the rules that bind us all, you have but one more attempt before she is as safe from you as she is from me. Make it a good one."

"Why should the Lord of Hell care about what happens to me? Or about one mortal in one city?"

"I don't care about you, Apollonius. As far as I'm concerned you can go to ... well, maybe not. But you can wander for all Eternity and be forever lost after that. But as for her ...

"Three times she's beaten me. She has stolen souls from me, one of whom was a close disciple, another flesh of my flesh. She has set loose in my realm a creature over whom I have no control. I hate all of His creations, but I hate Bianca Jones more than most. Corrupt her, destroy her, make her suffer and you can ask whatever you want of me."

"You know what I want."

"Of course." The one called Morningstar knew the base and secret desires of all. "What you've always wanted - Dominion. Destroy Jones and her city's protection ends. I will then gather my legions and openly attack. You will appear and seemingly drive me away. You will then be recognized as the new Messiah."

"And how, if you had another chance, would you destroy this

woman?'

"Well, there's this house."

***

It's going to rain, thought the man in the darkened room. My old wounds ache. Laughing to himself, he added, Of course, they hurt when it's not raining as well. The price of survival to an old age.

Old age, he never thought he'd make it that far. The games he played, the chances he took. He should have been dead years, no decades ago. Somehow he had always managed to avoid the one foe everyone must face and no one can defeat.

It was thanks to the women, he realized, that he had survived so long.

She Who Was had brought fire into his life.

Tyche had shared just enough luck to see him through difficult times.

Bianca Jones had fought at his side in a plague-ravaged land. Together they had become gods and together had renounced their divinity.

And there was Leda, Nemesis of evil, his own avenger in black. He had known her only briefly but had loved her all his days.

Days that were now numbered. He was down to only a few. Not even that, maybe. Twice this month his nurses had pulled him back from the brink. More women who had saved his life.

No more. This had been a good life but it was time to move on to the next one, it was time to maybe see Leda again. When the pains in his chest came he would not cry out. Instead he would laugh in the face of Death and dare him to do his worst.

With this vow in his mind and near silent laughter on his lips, Michael Shaw, whom some had called the Nightmare, drifted off to sleep.

And into the next world.

***

The House was just a house, DeWitt Jackson decided. No matter that there had been five people inside it when it first disappeared. Or that those who walked by the empty lot on which it had stood swore they heard screaming. Or that when the house first reappeared the bodies inside it had been killed fifty years before and two hundred miles away.

It was just a house.

Jackson had been through it twice. He had searched it thoroughly. He had been a cop, a damn good one. Still was, despite his circumstances. He knew how to conduct a search. And he could search places that no one else could.

So what if that TV crew had entered through the front door only to find themselves in Tulsa, Oklahoma? That at least had made Sergeant Bianca Jones laugh out loud, something she seldom did.

There was nothing in the house to suggest the supernatural. No blood dripping from the walls, no moving paintings, no unidentified noises. And no ghosts.

Definitely no ghosts.

Jackson was certain about that. He was sure he would recognize a ghost when he saw one. After all, it took one to know one.

He was about to leave when he got an idea. He was a ghost. He was in a vacant house. Maybe he could "haunt" it, possess it like he could possess people, something he'd done more than once.

Maybe not the best idea you've ever had, DeWitt, he told himself. What if you get stuck? What if the house decides to disappear again and takes you with it? What if …

He shut himself up. A good cop follows orders, and Sergeant Jones had ordered him to search the house. And while she hadn't been able to save his life she had saved his soul, and if she wanted the house searched that's exactly what he's do, to the best of his ability.

Taking a mental breath (the only kind he had left) and metaphorically closing his eyes, Jackson extended his senses, feeling the house, becoming one with it. The floors and walls became his bones, the plumbing his veins and arteries, the ancient wiring his nervous system.

And still it was nothing more than a house. There were mice in the walls, rats in the basement, and squirrels' nests in the attic insulation. There was nothing in this house that was not in other vacant houses that did not on occasion vanish. No spectral presence other than himself. No traces of any murder victims, present or past. There was noth …

Had he not just then been thinking of murder Jackson might have missed it. Something in the basement, something small, no more than three inches long.

Releasing the house, Jackson drifted through floors down to the basement. Looking at his find he asked himself, "Now then, how are you going to get it outside?"

***

Somehow she remembered it all. Her own power turned against her. The shattering of her bones and rupturing of her organs. She remembered the cold metal of the slab and the man who cut her open. He immediately sewed her up after declaring her "most sincerely dead."

The hardness of the wooden box and the smell of freshly dug earth. Then the darkness.

She had expected to wake by the River. Instead, Delilah Solomon, aka Mari Beverly Mercer, rotted in the ground. Her body dead, her mind alive, waiting in the dark.

She waited in the dark for the Bright One to release her and tell her her true name. When he did not she at first despaired. Had she placed her hopes and trust in a false god? Was it to be her fate to spend eternity in a limbo of darkness? Then she remembered that the Bright One was not a merciful deity. He rewarded only the strong and had only contempt for the weak.

And Delilah Solomon had failed her god. She had allowed the Jones woman to steal her powers and use them against her. She could expect no help from her god. If she was to be saved, she would have to save herself.

She was aware. That told Solomon that her power, although weak and mostly spent, had not completely faded. It was sustained by her belief in the Bright One and from her mind and her true self.

Solomon extended her consciousness. Wood encased her, the plain wood of her coffin, wood that, like her, had once been alive. She took what she could from it.

The earth that surrounded her was not itself alive, but it teemed with life. Insects and microbes within it, grass above it. Life that she could use, life she could steal.

Her power grew. She turned it inward and began to heal her body, to repair the damage done to it. When she was strong enough, she would dig upwards and return from the dead.

***

She should have killed me, Felix Manion thought, not for the first time. She was supposed to have killed me. It had been, he believed, her only choice.

The woman who had beaten him had proven him wrong. She had

faked his death, eliminating the need to try him for his crimes against the city she protected. She had hidden him in a prison under the name Edgar Payton, sentenced him to life for crimes he had not committed so that he might pay for the more horrible crimes of which he was guilty. She had not damned herself as had been planned.

It was a death of sorts, Manion supposed. Buried away, denied his own self, separated from all he knew. For all the world knew he was truly dead.

He knew, of course, that true death was only words away. His well-publicized crimes had been infamous, shocking all but the most hardened of terrorists. One slip, one hint of his real name and then would come the knife in the shower, the fatal beating in the dark, or the "accidental" fall from the catwalk circling the third tier where his cell was located.

There would be no investigation. There would be no punishment. His killer might even be given special privileges.

It was one way out the prison that held him. But it would be a useless death. It would not benefit the Bright One in any way. It would earn Manion no reward in the life after this.

One day the time would be right. One day the release promised him by his lord and master would come. Manion was a patient man. He could wait for that day.

***

"Where did you get this?" Bianca asked Officer Jackson as they sat in a back booth of the 10-44 Bar in South Baltimore. To the cop bar's other patrons the booth appeared to be empty and in many respects it was. Jackson ghostly presence was unseen and Bianca had walked through a dream to get there.

"Ask me how I got it here." Using his dream conjured beer as a pointer, Jackson indicated the newspaper-wrapped package that lay on the table between them. "That's a better story."

At Bianca's nod Jackson went on. "Did you know the mind of a rat is just as disgusting as the rest of it? Eating, crapping, sleeping, and screwing are all it thinks of?"

"So they're much like every guy I've ever met?" Bianca countered, with a mental exception for her husband Joe.

"Yeah, I guess I walked into that one. But a rat doesn't give its own ass about sports, so there's the difference. Anyway, I had to enter one's mind to get it to carry … that… outside. Then I had to snag the mind of one of the local dealers who are always hanging about the area so I could have him wrap it up and take it to the Southwest with instructions to deliver it to you."

"And when they saw what it was they arrested him."

"Yeah, but you got most of the charges dropped. It's not my fault he was holding."

Bianca unwrapped the package that her ghostly subordinate had retrieved from the house and looked at it once again. It appeared to be the shriveled remains of a human digit.

"I'll have Tammy run this for DNA and prints. See if we get a hit on who it belonged to. Thanks, DeWitt. Good job."

"My pleasure, Sarge. Always glad to give my commanding officer the finger."

***

The dirt of the unmarked grave crumbled and fell into itself. From out of the hole crawled something that could be described as human only in the most general of terms. Looking around, the body of what had been and what would be Delilah Solomon searched for sustenance.

Gunshots in the near distance. Solomon stumbled toward them on unsteady legs.

"You crazy, Lees, killing a body in a boneyard."

"Why not, Janes? This is where she gonna end up. Save the cops the … what the hell is that?"

"That" was the skeletal form of Delilah Solomon. Shots from both men struck her body, but it's difficult to kill what had once been dead.

Janes and Lees thought to run, but something held them fast. As the creature they thought existed only in comics and movies came closer, both men fouled themselves. If the creature minded, it didn't complain.

"You will do," it said in a rough voice that was a mixture of the Caribbean, New Orleans and the Outer Banks. "The three of you will do nicely."

Involuntarily, Janes and Lees looked down at their victim.

"She's not quite dead. Thank you for your poor marksmanship."

Then Solomon reached out with her power, found the living essence the two men and dying woman and drained it from them, her body filling out as theirs wasted away. When it was over,

"Shame you were such a skinny thing," Solomon said to the dried hulk of the dead woman. "I could have used your clothes. No matter."

Spending a small part of her power, she fashioned a plain blouse and skirt from the clothing of her victims. Then, once again herself, she left the cemetery to seek her master and do his bidding.

***

One day ran into the next, each one the same. No options, no choices. Manion waited in vain for deliverance, but it did not come. Finally, he realized that if he was to be freed, he would have to do it himself.

He became more involved with the prison community, talking to and learning about his fellow inmates. Playing off his manufactured reputation he let it be known that his services were available and soon was putting his planning ability and violent skills to use. He showed no preference, joined no gangs, worked for whoever could pay his price. The coins he dealt in were favors and information, which, in his hands, were deadlier than any weapon. Soon, he had enough.

He used the knowledge gained. He cashed in his favors. A name on the outside. A phone call made to that name. An assignment given. Finally, a piece of paper with a web address slipped to Warden Carl Robinson.

Robinson pulled up the website. One it were three videos. The first was one he had heard about but never seen. It depicted the brutal murders of a woman and her children. Murders ordered because their husband and father had made the wrong choice.

With a feeling of unease Robinson started the second video. It showed his mother outside her home. His sister entering the office building where she worked. His nephew leaving his school.

The third video was the same as the second, expect that it was intercut with scenes from the first. A voiceover recited the names and addresses of other members of his family.

Then came the choice. The prisoner named Edgar Payton was to be released within one hour from the day and time the current video ended, or Robinson's loved ones would become the subjects of a video much like the first.

One hour was not enough time to do all that was needed to protect his family. Robinson knew this and let his heart and his fear make the choice for him. He had Payton brought to his office.

"There's a secret exit from this facility to the outside," he told the prisoner. "It's so the staff can be evacuated in case of a severe prison uprising."

"I'll need a gun," Manion told him.

Robinson shook his head. "That wasn't part of the choice."

"You're right, it wasn't. My fault. But I could use your coat, to cover my jumpsuit. You wouldn't want me getting caught."

Robinson gave Manion his coat and led him to the emergency exit.

Before he left Manion told him, "You made the right choice. Your family will be safe. You have the word of Felix Manion." Then he was gone.

Robinson knew the name. Knew what horrible things had been done in that name. Back in his office, he waited out the time until the evening count, when Payton would be missed. There would be an investigation and his part in the escape would come to light. He could only hope that the law he helped enforce would understand the choice he had to make.

***

Their business over, Bianca left Jackson to watch whatever game the perpetually on television was playing and used her dream to take her home where she planned to spend a quiet evening with her husband Joe. Well, maybe not so quiet, she thought, thinking about the sighs, moans and other exclamations of delight she envisioned the two of them making before falling into a deep, satisfied sleep.

However, when she emerged from her lucid dreaming state the look on Joe's face told her that this was not to be. His next words confirmed it.

"Beth called."

Joe's voice carried the disappointment and loneliness of a loving husband who spent far too many night alone and the worry that one night would be the night she did not return and that he'd be alone the rest of his life.

"Three dead at St. Elizabeth's Cemetery. Newly dead," he said quickly then added, "and one open grave and a missing body."

"Please tell me that it isn't …"

"Beth woke the caretaker up. He's checking the grave records now. But who else could it be?'

"Damn. Next time we burn her to ashes then scatter the ashes."

Bianca looked at her husband, her patient, understanding husband. Like she was, he had once been with the BPD. He knew all about working nights, lost weekends, and cancelled plans. It didn't make things any easier.

Suddenly she was tempted to say to hell with it all, to let Beth Steele and the rest of what had become known as The Freak Show handle this one without her – just for the night. Tomorrow would be time enough to catch up, to start the witch hunt.

Though he would never tell Bianca, there were times when Joe could read his wife as easily as one of the books he sold in his shop. He knew what she was thinking, knew that whatever pleasure she might derive from not answering Detective Steele's call would be repaid three times over in guilt and recrimination over the next several days.

"Go," he said softly. "I'll wait up. We can have breakfast in bed."

Bianca smiled at the one good thing in her life. Then she went out into the night.

***

"It's her," Beth Steele said as soon as Bianca arrived. "The caretaker confirmed it."

"I think an open grave and three shriveled husks of what used to be human beings confirm it. That bitch is back. Now tell me the rest of the bad news."

When Beth hesitated Bianca went on. "Beth, you're too good a detective not to have already taken the next step. What's the word on Manion?"

Beth confirmed Bianca's suspicions. "He's gone. The warden was given a choice. He chose his family."

Of course he did, Bianca thought, trying not to condemn the man for making a choice she might one day soon have to make. She thought of all the people she'd gotten close to since taking on the role of Baltimore's defender against that which lurks in the darkness of the night and the soul. If Manion wasn't stopped they'd be used against her, and she against them. She started thinking of ways to keep that from happening.

"He'll be coming here," she said, "and teaming with the witch. The prefect couple."

Bianca looked over the crime scene, saw what she needed to. "Tomorrow morning, everyone in my office. Have the Medical Examiner burn those," she indicated the three bodies, "once they're ID'd. And have the lab get a couple of cans of dirt from the grave."

"Why would we need that?" Beth asked.

Bianca shrugged. "I have no idea. It's a just hunch. But it can't hurt and might help."

Having done all she could do, Bianca drove home to Joe. She found him asleep in front of the television which had stopped playing the DVD he had put in. She woke him up, got him into bed, and fell asleep next to him. The next morning over breakfast – in bed – she told him everything. Then, dishes cleared, they stayed in bed just a little longer. Afterwards they held each other as if it might be their last time together, both of them aware that one day it just might be.

***

They had all seen the video, more than once. The one that Warden Robinson had watched. Bianca made her team view it again.

As her team watched the brutality on the screen she watched them, knowing what they were thinking. What if that were me? What, who would my friends sacrifice to save me? Or would I be sacrificed for the greater good? What if it's my choice? Could I, would I condemn my loved ones to save strangers.

"Those are the stakes. I'd ask if anyone wants to back out but that option isn't open. We'll have to assume that the witch can find us, wherever we are. Then Manion gives us the choice."

Lieutenant Tavon Greggs spoke up. "So we find them first and don't give them an option. We kill them quick, burn the bodies, and scatter the ashes."

Before Bianca could reply to the Criminalist Tammy Dolan said, "If they're even in the city. They may target someplace else."

There was more than a trace of hope in the civilian's voice that this cup might pass from them. Of them all, she was the least experienced. Like Joe, Tammy had never been on the front lines of this war. After Joe, Bianca worried about her the most.

"The Feds are on the alert, Tammy. So is the DMA. If they're found, when they're found, we all go after them."

Again she looked at her crew, her Freak Show as they had begun to be called. And again, as she had some time ago, she wondered how this assortment of people had come together and why they continually risked their lives and souls to fight evils and horrors most people would deny even existed.

Bianca answered her own question. Because we can. Because no one else will.

"So what's the plan, Chief?" Greggs asked.

"Basic investigative techniques. We know the MO, we look for crimes that fit it. Manion may start small, keep off the radar. The witch might be able to shield him. Joe, can you track either using their DNA and sympathetic magic?"

"Won't that alert Solo ..."

"Not the name, Beth."

"Sorry, Bianca. Won't that alert the witch that we're after her."

"She's evil, not stupid. She knows. Joe?"

"I've tried, Bianca, but," Joe shook his head, "no luck. Looks like the DNA was a one time trick. She's somehow managed to block me. Or she used what she took from those three bodies to change it."

"Damn." Bianca nodded as if she had expected that. "Anyway, safety first. Speaking of tracking, Joe has something for each of us."

Joe handed each of them a small charm. "Each of these has a twin, which means they can be traced. If anyone is taken, these might help us get to them in time. But if we can't ..." He passed out envelopes. "Inside these is a word. Read it, memorize it, burn it. Do not speak it aloud."

"What's it for," Tammy asked, knowing she was not going to like the answer.

Tavon supplied it. "It's a suicide pill."

Joe nodded in confirmation. "Something like that. If you're taken and they, well, you reach your limit, say the word and you will cease to be, and so will everyone around you."

"What about any nearby innocents?"

"Where you'd be taken, Tammy, there won't be any innocents." Bianca then turned so as to address them all. "One more thing. If you're taken, we will do our best to save you. But any choice is no choice at all. Our duty is to protect the people of Baltimore. Understood?"

They all nodded. Dismissed, they filed out, Beth and Tavon to work out tactics, Joe and Tammy to discuss forensic techniques that might aid in finding Solomon and Manion.

After they left ...

Harsh, Sarge, said a voice inside her head.

"Had to be said, DeWitt."

When you gonna tell them about me?

"You're my ace in the hole. Joe knows. As for the others, the less they know, they less they can tell. You know how it is. How it has to be."

I know, Sarge. Maybe when this is over.

***

Her telephone was ringing when Bianca got back to her office. It was Security.

"Sargent Jones. This is Winder at the President Street entrance. I've got a man here who says that he has a package for you. The box is long and narrow and while nothing shows up on the scan he says it's a knife."

"What's his name?"

"He says it's Moran."

A name from the past. Both the long past and one not so far removed. She would have thought him dead, but his kind were long lived.

"Is his first name Seamus and how tall is he compared to me?"

This was an unfair question. It was well know that Bianca Jones was sensitive about her height. Anyone mentioning her lack of it was apt to face her wrath, a wrath that had been successfully turned against monsters, demons, and federal officers. Officer Winder's reply was delayed as he searched for the words that would not get him transferred to permanent night shift and finally said, "Yes, his name is Seamus and he's… er … a few inches less tall than you, Sergeant."

Winder's answer and the prospect of seeing Seamus Moran again gave Bianca reasons to smile on an otherwise bleak day.

"Have him escorted up, Officer. Good job."

The compliment from Bianca Jones gave Officer Winder his own reason to smile that day. He hated night shift.

Seamus Moran. He was one of the Gentry, the Fair Folk. Decades ago he had owned a New York bar, one that after hours had hosted men and women who wore dark colors and fought even darker evil. She had last seen him in a mythical land that was all too real. She had heard from his cousin that he had closed the bar and returned to that land.

And now he was back.

Bianca could think of only one reason for his return. And why he would be bringing her a knife.

Bianca waited for the man some would have called a leprechaun to sit down and take his first sip of the coffee she had poured before saying,

"He's dead, isn't he?"

"Aye, lass, he is. He passed away a few days ago."

"Did he … die well?"

Seamus smiled and nodded. "Michael Shaw, whom some called the Nightmare and whom many called friend died of advanced old age and, I suspect, boredom as a result of that old age. He lived longer than he should have, having been touched far too often by legend, myth, and magic. There's some of that in you, Lady Bán."

Again Bianca thought back to the mythical land of Eire, the soul of Ireland and Moran's birthplace. To save that land she and the Nightmare had taken on the aspects of gods, aspects which they both ultimately rejected.

"He left this with me, to give to you when his time came."

Seamus handed her the package. Almost reverently, Bianca opened it. As she had expected, it contained the long fighting knife he had picked up in Eire. She had had ones like it, but had left them with her godhood on bloody ground after too much slaughter.

Picking it up, Bianca found that it fit naturally in her palm, as if it had accepted her. With less reluctance than she would have supposed, she, in turn, accepted it and wondered just what effect a possibly enchanted knife from Eire might have on a certain witch.

Seamus's voice broke into her thoughts.

"Before giving it to me, he had it inscribed."

Bianca examined the blade. On one side was engraved *Tromluí*, the name Shaw had adopted in Eire. How like him to name his weapon after himself, she thought. One the other side Shaw had had etched, *Am a Imirt*. Bianca did not need to speak Gaelic to know that it meant "Time to play."

"Unlike others of his kind, Michael never embraced the darkness in which he fought. Like them he laughed but sometimes that laughter was from the sheer joy of being allowed to do something worthwhile."

Still holding the knife – her knife now– Bianca said, "To me it's not a game. It's a serious business, with serious consequences. And Tromluí here could do some damage to those who deserve it. Thank you, Seamus."

The small man, if man he ever was, got up and after taking Bianca's hand, prepared to leave. Then,

"Ah, I must be getting old. I almost forgot. He left this for you as well."

From his coat he produced a small, wrapped package. Then despite her requests for him to stay – "Thank you, lass, but this is no longer my world, if it ever was. The sooner I'm back home to the better" – he took his leave.

"Lady Bán."

To his formal bow she raised Tromluí in a fencer's salute. "Master Moran."

Another bow and Seamus Moran turned clockwise from reality and was gone.

"At least I don't have to escort him out," she said to herself as she opened to package.

It was an old digest-sized pulp magazine the fading colors of which proclaimed,

"From the Shadows – featuring a full length adventure of the Nightmare and The Phoenix."

The cover showed an artist's rendition of the Nightmare in black. Beside him was a blazing woman who seemed to be part bird, her hair and costume all the colors of the flame. Side by side they faced a man sitting on a throne and dressed in white. Below them were the words,

"In this issue the Man in Black and She Who Is face the Bright One in a battle for Manhattan."

The Bright One. A man in white. On a throne. Just like in Eire. Suddenly it came together and Bianca knew just who and what she was facing. She found and gripped her knife, knowing that the Nightmare's gift would be useful in her battle for Baltimore.

***

"Apollonius, that crazy bastard who tried to take over Eire. I should have figured it out."

Bianca was raving up and down the aisles of Morgan's Books, her husband Joe's book store. Like a good husband he tried make her feel better.

"There was no way you could have known."

"I should have considered it, allowed for the possibility." Bianca was angry, more at herself than anyone else. But it was Joe who caught the brunt of that anger. So like any smart husband he knew just to be quiet and continue to peruse the books in the back room of the shop, a back room that, judging from the exterior of the store, had no business being there.

Finally calming down, Bianca looked over at Joe, loving him for his patience and understanding and hoping he wouldn't test that love by saying anything but what she needed to hear. Wisely, Joe kept his head down and began to read from a book he had pulled from a shelf.

"Apollonius of Tyana lived in the first century C.E. His was a miraculous birth and when he came of age he became a preacher and philosopher and was believed to have performed such wonders as healing the sick, raising the dead, and casting out demons. He was betrayed to the Romans and died shortly thereafter. However, his followers claimed that he returned from the dead."

Joe looked up from the book. "Sound like anyone you've heard of?"

Before Bianca could reply he read on. "There are records of his appearing in other lands such as India and the Caliphate." "And Eire and Gotham," Bianca added. "He's died at least three times. Between Shaw and me we've killed him twice. What does it take?"

Joe knew the answer, did not want to say it or even think it. To kill a god took great magic, more magic than might be contained in a Fairie blade. And all magic has a price. And from what Bianca had told him of Eire, she and the Nightmare had come close to paying it there. And if the pulp magazine that Moran had given her was to be believed, Shaw had paid it again, only to be saved by love and the Spirit of the City.

He looked over at Bianca. The woman he loved was lost in her mind, making plans to kill a god, stop his minions, and save her city. Suddenly she turned and looked at him. In her eyes were tears and determination. She too knew the price of magic.

"It's what we do, Joe."

He nodded, tried to smile, then together they began to make plans.

***

Bianca filled in her team the next day.

"We're facing a being who has the power level of a god. Or at least the son of a god. He's already tried to destroy a part of Fairie and New York City. He uses violence and disease to do it and brings in mercenaries from other times to help him. Any questions or suggestions."

"Let him come and bring as many friends as he's got," Greggs said defiantly. "Back before we first dealt with that witch you told us to prepare for damned near anything, especially the dammed things. Well, I've got the ammo and I've got the guns, and I've got contacts inside some of the gangs. You know how much they hate visiting teams coming into Birdland and setting up. Say the word and pick the targets and I'll turn them loose."

Bianca had expected Beth to object to using Baltimore's not-quite-organized criminals but the homicide detective just shrugged and said,

"The way this city's been lately, a little more violence won't even be noticed. Hell, a lot more violence wouldn't be noticed. Besides, sending killers after killers seems like a workable idea."

Bianca wasn't sure she liked how the conversation was going. She remembered what Nietzsche had written,

"Whoever fights monsters should see to it that in the process he does not become a monster."

They had each of them fought their share of monsters – human and otherwise – and had so far retained their humanity. The saving of Baltimore might be worth their lives, but not their souls.

"Let's save that as the last resort. Instead, Tavon, contact the State Police, the FBI, the reserves and the National Guard. Mention Terrorism and Manion's name in the same breath. That should get their attention. Joe, Tammy, where are we on the disease threat?"

"The CDC and NIH are on alert and ready to handle anything natural," Tammy replied. "As for anything else, we've got the DMA and several spiritual healers on standby. Like the lieutenant said, let 'em come."

"Two of them are already here and I want them taken out before their boss shows up. Joe, you keep trying to locate them magically. Meanwhile, the Commissioner has agreed to give us as many interns, light duties, limited duties, and cops serving administrative suspensions as can be spared. They are going to be checking every report that comes in looking for anything with even a whiff of the unnatural or extortion by violence. If they do, Tavon and Beth will take tactical teams to check it out."

And I'll be watching the spirit plane for the same thing, Sarge.

Good man, DeWitt.

I was once and hope to be again.

***

As the Freak Show made their plans, Felix Manion was busy advancing his master's cause. As always, he was offering choices and making deals.

No terrorism this time. That had been merely to attract attention, to get the Jones bitch to condemn herself by her own actions. This time the Bright One needed soldiers.

No need to bring in mercenaries this time, his master had decided.

There were enough of the disaffected in the city that an army easily could be raised. Recruit from the gangs, Manion was told. They were already loosely organized, violent, well-armed and had displayed a definite contempt for the laws of gods and men.

As a white skinned man with white-blonde hair walking the streets of the inner city asking about drug gangs and their leaders, it did not take long before Manion was noticed.

The first two dealers he approached believed him to be a Fed and wanted nothing to do with him. The next one reported Manion's presence to his gang's enforcer, who sent three of his crew to mess Manion up and find out his game. They came back without their guns and cash but with a broken wrist each.

And with an offer. Join the Bright One. Take the money he was offering. Become part of his army and recruit others on his behalf. Rise up when the call comes out. Kill police, community leaders, elected officials. Bomb public buildings and institutions. Cause chaos that will bring the city down and allow the Bright One to claim it for himself.

Do all this and Baltimore and its people will be yours.

Fail to join and become part of the hunted.

The Gwynn Oak Ninjas listened to what Manion offered. So did the Clifton Park Crewe and several other gangs. To some it seemed like a good idea. To others it was just another government plot to get them in one place and take them all out at once. Still others remembered weeks of terror and an Internet video of a woman and child being savaged and murdered.

Phone calls were made. Texts were exchanged. An agreement was reached. Manion was called and given a time and place.

"Be there," he was told. "Be alone."

***

Reports of the weird, strange, and coerced criminality had begun appearing on Bianca's desk. All needed to be checked out, a task too much for Beth Steele and Tavon Greggs. Major Pompey Fredericks, commander of the BPD's Homicide Unit, detailed some investigators and the District Detective Units were each required to assign someone. Bianca was about to pick up some case folders and hit the streets when the Commissioner's office called.

"Sergeant Jones," said the only person in the BPD who could give

Bianca orders and expect them to be followed, "What do you know about Genny Starr?"

Bianca thought for a moment. "Latest pop sensation. More wholesome than Disney. Why?"

"She called my office personally. She's in trouble and says only you can help."

"Sir, as you know I'm very busy right now with …"

"I am aware of your activities, Sergeant." (Not good, Bianca thought, he's not using contractions.) But I think the Freak Show can get along without you while you see what America's latest sweetheart needs."

With a "Damn, now the name's official" to herself, the only thing for Bianca to say was "Yes, Sir" and ask for the details.

"It's probably a trap," Beth told Bianca over a drink at Frank's Hall, their favorite, and closest, cop bar.

"Probably," agreed Bianca. "The most wholesome singer since Doris Day, one with absolutely no breath of scandal about her, the girl whose idea of a hot date is holding hands at a PG movie, suddenly calls for my help. Yeah, it's a trap of some kind."

"Manion's gotten to her, threatening to murder her family or expose a sordid past unless she sets you up. Why else would the meeting be out of town?"

"I can think of one reason, Beth, and it has nothing to do with the Bright One. Call Tavon, I'll need some of his men as backup."

***

A rest stop off I95 south of Baltimore. There at an outside table, sipping a cola was America's blue-eyed, blonde haired darling. Every boy's ideal wife, every girl's best friend. Mothers wished their daughters could be like her. Father's looked at their wives and … just wished. She was of course wearing a dress that would suggest but not reveal a no doubt perfect figure.

Bianca Jones, who had no figure at all, and had seen and done too much in her life to have any claim on the innocence Genny Starr epitomized, walked over to her.

"Miss Starr," (Genny insisted on Miss, not Ms.) "I'm Bianca Jones. My Commissioner said you needed my help."

Genny Starr looked at Bianca. Then what might have been the bluest eyes in the world began to tear up. "I'm sorry to have brought you here,

Miss Jones, but I …"

The bluest eyes in world darkened, and Genny's sweet voice deepened.

"But she really didn't have much of a choice."

Despite the lovely shape before her, despite the sound of her voice, Bianca knew the speaker. It was someone she had encountered before, someone who because of those encounters could not be present – physically or spiritually – inside her city. Bianca looked into the bluest eyes in the world and saw Evil.

"Morningstar," she said, mentally reviewing the words Joe had taught her for just such a meeting. If need be she'd use them, even if meant her death and that of America's Girlfriend, if it was the only way to send Satan back to Hell.

"Frist of all, Ms. Jones," the creature now in control of Genny Starr said, "let me assure you that I plan to take no adverse action against you or the …" he stopped to count "… four armed officers you have hidden nearby, or the spirit who is hovering close above me, although the marks on his soul makes him almost as much mine as yours. I am here with an offer, a warning, or at least a message."

"You'll forgive me if I don't believe you."

"It not my job to forgive anyone, Ms. Jones, but I do understand. And before we get down to business I'll answer the obvious question. Once upon a time there was a young girl who was nothing special. I'm sure you remember what that was like. But instead of working hard for what she wanted, she made a wish, a wish for a perfect life. And someone heard her and offered to grant that wish. Unfortunately for her, it was not a genie, nor was it the Blue Fairy. It was, well, you know."

Lucifer paused, took a sip of the cola, and made a face. He gestured, took another sip, and smiled.

"Better. He's not the only one who can change beverages, although I prefer rum. Now where were we? Oh yes, a bargain was made. No, I did not ask for her soul, I have more than enough of them, people give them to me all the time. No, instead I asked only for a day of her life. Now I'm sure that the little nothing that would become Genny Starr thought that this meant she would die on a Tuesday instead of a Wednesday or something like that. But … that's not the case, is it, Genny?'

At this question Genny's eyes returned to their natural blue. Bianca saw pleading in them and knew that the young woman was conscious and fully aware of what was happening and what would happen to her.

"But to business, Ms. Jones. Apollonius of Tyana, the self-styled Bright One, has again resurrected and is in your city. He does not mean to destroy it. In fact, he finds it charming. No, he means to destroy you. I can understand his feelings. Once you're destroyed, he plans to use Baltimore as his base to take over as much of the world as he can. I doubt he'll get far, but any destruction he causes is good for business, my business."

"Why come to me?" Bianca asked.

"As I said, an offer. Allow me and mine back in Baltimore and allow me a certain freedom to operate, and I'll take down Apollonius for good."

Bianca shook her head. "Go back to Hell. I'll be sending Apollonius there to meet you soon."

Satan smiled. "Pride is my most deadly sin as well, Ms. Jones. So, some advice, given freely and without obligation. Trust no one. Even He had his betrayers and doubters."

"You spoke of a message."

"Yes, I did. The Bright One offers you a choice. You can come after him and his with all your resources, your Freak Show, that godmaker Richards, the DMA, and the rest, and Armageddon will come to Baltimore. People will die, your friends first, you last."

Bianca knew what was coming. Still she asked, "Or?"

"Or you face them alone, just you against the Bright One and his current allies. Do this and your friends and comrades will be spared. When you fall, if you fall, they will be alive to carry on the fight."

"And if I choose not to believe him?"

"As you know, I am a stickler for contracts. I will be watching Apollonius very carefully. Should he renege in any way, ban or no ban I will come after him and drag him down to the Circle of Betrayers."

"What's in it for you?"

"If you win, I'm rid of a potential opponent. I've enough trouble with one Messiah, let alone two. If Apollonius wins, at the very least I'm rid of you."

"Let me think about it."

"Really, Ms. Jones. I'm the one who tells the lies. You have thought about it. It's all you've thought about. We both know your answer, don't we?"

He was right. Bianca had always know it would come down to her against the Bright One. It had been just her and the Nightmare in Eire, the Nightmare alone in New York. Now it was her turn.

Slowly, she nodded.

"You have time, twenty-four hours in fact." Using the sweetest face in the country again Satan smiled. "I plan to be busy the rest of the day. And tonight there will be pictures and videos to post."

Twenty-four hours. Only one day to prepare. There was no time to waste. She should leave, except …

Bianca looked into the face America had fallen in love with, knowing that by tomorrow this time Genny Starr would be a fallen idol, a joke or two on every late night talk show, another young girl gone bad, and proof that there was no longer anything like goodness left in this world.

America and the world could take care of itself. They had had their hopes dashed before and would again. It was Genny Bianca was most worried about. The young woman was about to be shamed and degraded, subjected to the worse kinds of sexual assault and abuse. And no one would know save those at the table where they sat. Instead Genny would become a public joke, a dirty punchline, an image to be downloaded by millions to satisfy their carnal desires.

And there was nothing Bianca could do about it. A deal had been made, a contract struck and agreed to. Bianca could see no way to save Genny, not without putting herself and all that she loved at risk. That she would not do, not for a foolish girl who thought she could play with Hellfire and walk away with an unburnt soul. Genny Starr's was one soul that she would not be able to steal from the Devil.

Lucifer knew this. There were other ways he could have conveyed his offer and message. Instead, he had set this meeting up to claim this victory over her, to watch her sitting helpless before him.

Still, Bianca never was one to graciously accept defeat.

"I'd like to help you, Genny," Bianca said to the woman trapped inside her own body, "but I can't. It was your choice to deal with the Devil and now you're going to have face the consequences of that choice."

By the cock of his head, the smile on his lips, and the darkness in his eyes, Bianca could tell that Satan was enjoying this. Then she said,

"There is a Higher Power over us. Whatever happens today, tomorrow, or the days after that, when it gets too much for you to bear, turn to Him, ask for help and forgiveness. If you are truly repentant, you will be forgiven and your soul saved."

"A feeble effort, Ms. Jones, but one I suppose you had to make."

"I was talking to you both." A look of surprise crossed the face of Genny Starr. "Yes, even you, Morningstar, if you ever swallow that Pride of yours. Only then can you again be an angel and stop bullying little girls for cheap thrills. What about it? Say the Words, mean the Words, and I'll grant you absolution myself. It won't be the first time I've done that."

When the Devil stayed silent, Bianca stood. "Genny, if you are truly sorry then your sins are forgiven. May God be with you and protect you."

Quickly, Bianca turned and walked away. As she did so she thought she heard someone using Genny Starr's voice say, "Well I'll be damned – again."

***

On the night of the day Bianca dealt with the Devil, Manion arrived at his own meeting on an athletic field behind what was once a public school but was now just another vacant building.

At the given time he waved a flashlight three times.

No answering light. Perhaps he was early. No, if anything the gangs would have spotters carefully hidden to make sure that he had come alone, that this was not an elaborate ruse by the authorities.

He waved his flash again. Still no answer. Fools, he thought, why would they not want money and power? It was the natural choice. It was the human choice.

The thought of betrayal crossed his mind. He dismissed it. If the gangs had wanted to do anything to him they had had their chance several times over.

Deciding they were playing with him, showing him who had the upper hand, he tried again. This time his flash was answered.

The bright lights of the athletic field came on, blinding him and revealing him to whoever was in darkness behind them.

I may have been wrong about betrayal, he thought, but then put the lights down to more intimidation. I can deal with that.

"Felix Manion." A voice from the surrounding darkness called out his name, his true name, the name he had never given any of the gangs.

"This is the police," the voice said unnecessarily. Manion stood stock still as the voice continued. "Yes, the gangs, some of them, gave you up. Their kind of crime requires order to flourish, not the chaos you offered. And while they're quite willing, sometimes all too eager to take out a snitch or competitor, some of them draw the line at torturing women and children. In short, you've been dimed out."

I've failed the master again, Manion thought as he raised his hands in surrender. This time, he knew, there would be no rescue, no escape.

He was more right than he thought.

Lieutenant Tavon Greggs stood in the darkness and carefully considered what he was about to do. How did I get here, he asked himself. One step at a time, was the answer, each step a choice whether a conscious one or not. And now one more step, over a line that could not be recrossed.

We fight monsters, he reminded himself for the third time in ten minutes, and Tavon Greggs knew only one way to do that.

His voice from the darkness was the last Felix Manion would hear in this world.

"Do it," came the order, then Greggs and several carefully chosen members of the QRT, all of whom had watched a certain video before setting up in ambush, opened fire without any moral qualms or regrets.

***

Returning to her office and trying not to think of what Genny Starr might be going through, Bianca prepared for war. She created assignments for her team, assignments that seemed legitimate but would serve to get them out of the city and remove them from harm's way. She cleaned and readied her weapons – her favorite shotgun with its flechette loads, two pistols – 9mm and .40 caliber, a back-up revolver, and, of course, the Nightmare's legacy, Tromluí. She picked it up from her desk. With her small frame it seemed more like a sword. She liked how it fit her hand.

Whatever else happens, a knife always works.

And with this thought a small, forgotten part of her soul stirred.

Before Bianca could notice, there was first a phone call. It was Greggs. His voice was flat, official.

"Manion's off the table."

"Tavon, what did you do?"

"What you've always done, the hard thing, the thing that needed doing."

She wisely asked no questions but briefly thought of hunting monsters.

Tammy Dolan then burst into her office with Joe right behind her. Both obviously had news and immediately began a game of "You first, no you, no you" which Bianca put an end to by saying,

"Joe, what do you have?"

"A way of using that graveyard dirt, a really nasty way." He told her what it was.

"Good job, get as many as you can ready by the end of the day. And what do you have Tammy?"

"The DNA results came back on that finger that dealer turned in." Tammy paused for effect. She always had been a little dramatic. At Bianca's "get on with it" she said, "It belongs to Bryan Knox, that boy from the video you showed us."

Bianca said, "Good job" and then was silent.

The House, of course. That was to be the battleground, where they would be found. Tomorrow morning she was to charge in, guns blazing, to cut down the Bright One's minions before facing the witch and finally Apollonius himself.

That was what the Nightmare would do. That's what they expect me to do. Don't they know that all houses, even this one, has a back door?

"Sergeant Jones?"

Tammy voice interrupted her thoughts.

"Sorry, Tammy, Joe. When this is over I'll need a vacation. As I said, good job, both of you. Now I have one more job for you. Check out a car. Drive to New York and look for a rainbow. Follow it to a bar. When you get there ask for Paddy Moran. You'll know him right away, he's shorter than I am. Tell him everything. He'll know what to do."

Tammy was confused, but she's gotten used to strange orders from her boss. She left to get ready. Joe stayed behind.

"You're sending us to safety, aren't you?"

"Maybe," she replied.

"I'm staying with you."

"Joe, my darling. I can't do what I have to do if I'm worried about you and the rest. I'm sending the whole Freak Show away. The day after tomorrow it will all be over, or will have just started. Today I failed. Tomorrow I may again. But at least I'll know I left others to continue the fight to save our city."

"I can't leave you, Bianca."

"And you never will, Joe. And I will never leave you. One way or the other I'll find my way back to you. Or you'll find your way to me. Now, before you and Tammy head north, there's one or two more jobs I need you to do. And if I'm right, the second one might be the hardest thing you've ever had to do. If I'm wrong, then take Tammy to New York and find that rainbow."

***

That night, alone in her house, Bianca lay in her bed. She was fully dressed in boots, battle dress pants and a pullover sweater. She wore a belt that had a pistol on one side and Tromluí on the other. At her right side was a shotgun with really nasty shells. At her left was a bag containing extra ammunition and weapons. She was ready for war. She was ready for sleep.

***

It was late evening when Joe and Tammy set out. She'll be settling in soon, he thought. Drifting into lucid sleep, walking what someone had once called the dream plane. He wished he could be with her, if only to watch over her in her sleep. But he had a job to do, and Bianca had been right. It was the hardest thing she had ever asked of him.

"I thought we were going to New York," Tammy said as Joe merged on to I495N towards Philadelphia.

"Change of plans," was all he said at first. Then, "The law of similarity. Have you ever heard of it?"

"Something to do with magic. I've heard you mention it once or twice."

Joe nodded. "Like calls to like. It was the first real magic I learned. Before we left, Bianca asked me to use the law to compare the finger from the House against the same DNA you used to make your match. My results were very different from yours."

Joe paused. Tammy stayed silent and he continued.

"What was offered? What choice were you given?"

Tammy's reply came haltingly, her voice strained. Yet in it was same relief, as if she glad to rid of the secret.

"I have … a brother. He has a family – wife, three kids. They were … threatened, you know how, if I didn't … lead Bianca to the House. I didn't see the harm, we … she was looking for the Bright One anyway. This led her to him."

"Yes," Joe said. "You led her to him. It was, it is a trap and you led her into it. And yes, she knew it was a trap, she thinks everything is a trap. But if she hadn't asked herself why that finger was found where it was, she would have gone into the trap with less information that she has now."

Joe wanted to turn and look at Tammy, but needed to keep his eyes on the road. He kept driving and stared straight ahead.

"You should have spoken up. We would have protected you and your family. Laid our own trap. Instead you betrayed us, Tammy. Betrayed Baltimore and the people you once swore to protect."

"Wha … what's going to happen to me?"

"If it were any of the others, nothing pleasant. The way she feels now, Bianca would likely use you as bait. Fortunately, she left it up to me. There's a prison in north Philadelphia that most people think is closed. In reality, it's used to house the kind of 'people' the Freak Show and others like us fight. You'll be held there until this is all over."

Tammy nodded, more to herself than to Joe. It was, she admitted, more than she deserved. "And afterwards?"

"If there is an afterwards, that will be up to Bianca."

"She'll understand why I did it, won't she?"

"She understands," Joe said softly, "more than most, I think. She may even forgive you. But don't expect her to trust you. That you'll have to earn back."

A few hours later, Joe drove into New York alone. He followed the rainbow and found the bar. And as he waited anxiously to be called back home he kept asking himself, "How did they know about the House?"

***

Bianca slept. Bianca dreamed.

She dreamed of a house with 21 rooms, ten to a side and one at the end of a very long hall. Each room with a door. Behind those doors could be anything, or any thing. Some led to rooms that were other people's dreams. Behind others were nightmares best kept locked away. One door led Bianca to the 10-44. Another to a bedroom where a woman in black would eternally rock a baby that would never be hers.

The room at the end was where Bianca had once kept a monster, until she had invited it into her own soul. It had stayed with her until she left it on the Plains of Hell. A gift for Morningstar he had yet to appreciate.

This was her dream, her House of 21 doors. Over time she would remake it until each room was hers. She picked a room she knew was otherwise unoccupied. She opened its door …

And stepped into the basement of a house, a house she had never been inside. Still she knew it. It was the House. The House that disappeared and returned, taking some people away and returning others. The House where DeWitt had found the finger that was definitely not Bryan Knox's but rather bait.

Bianca asked herself the same question Joe was asking, "How had they known?" She had been asking herself that question and while she had not come to any conclusion, she did have some troubling suspicions.

Unlike DeWitt, Bianca could not phase through the basement ceiling to the floors above.

Why not, she asked, I'm in a dream.

But she was also now in the House, a place rooted in the real world, and certain physical laws did apply. Still, she was able to extend her dream sense throughout the House, and yes, it was occupied – Apollonius, Solomon, and about a dozen shades that the House had drawn to itself, shade of souls that the House had claimed, shades made solid by the Bright One to serve him.

Your bullets, blessed by the Church or not, will have no effect on the dead, a voice in her head told her. It was her voice, yet it was not.

Who are you? Bianca asked.

You know. And Bianca did. It was a part of her that she thought had left in Eire, a spirit of vengeance, a part of that had awakened when she accepted Tromluí. It was a spirit of vengeance, now with just a touch of Nightmare.

They know you are here. They await you. You cannot hope to defeat them.

But you can?

We can. Open yourself to me, and let them fear us.

Bianca worried about another trap, The Bright One knew of Bán and Tromluí. He had used them against her and Shaw. He could be using Bán again. It was something a mad god would do.

And that thought reminded Bianca that she was fighting a god. And the best weapon against a god was another god, and faith in that god, and faith in The God and faith in herself.

Bianca dropped her bag of spare ammo. She holstered the pistol she had drawn. On reflection, she undid her gun belt and laid that with the bag. Then armed only with her Mossberg, (she would have felt naked without it, and she did have a use for it), Tromluí, and her faith, she climbed the stairs.

The door from the stairs opened into a small hall between the kitchen and front entrance. From where she stood, she could see the ghosts of the

House staring at the front and back doors, waiting for her to come though one or the other. As she stepped into the hall, they turned toward her, as if alerted to her presence.

Slowly, they advanced.

Time to play, Bianca thought, drawing Tromluí and accepting Bán as part of herself.

Ghosts can be hurt, ghosts can bleed, ghosts can be killed again.

With the right weapon.

Wielded by one who was once a god and was close to being one again,

Tromluí was such a weapon.

The shades used their hands, feet, and teeth against her, Bianca slashed and stabbed them, her speed and her reflexes enhanced by Bán. She took wounds, none were fatal. Blood spattered her, none was hers. She lost count of her opponents, she lost track of time, she lost her sense of self in the battle against the ghosts of the House.

Then all stopped. No one came against her. Bán receded and Bianca was again herself. She looked around the first floor – the entry way, the kitchen, the living room. The bodies of her foes were all about. All were stabbed, some were missing limbs, others eviscerated.

Unlike on the fields of Temair, where stood Eire's Stone of Destiny, Bianca did not drop her knife and ask what she had done. She knew the answer. It was what she had always done, the hard thing, the thing that needed doing.

And there was more to do. Tired, battered, and bruised, Bianca climbed the stairs to the second floor.

She met her in the upstairs hall. Delilah Solomon, charms braided into her hair, her clothing a quilt of bright colors.

"Again we meet, small one. And again you are not a guest in this house, the house of the Bright One."

"And again I make you the same offer. Join with me and live. Oppose me and die. And this time there will be no return, for your Bright One will soon join you in Hell. Choose, Mari Beverly Mercer," Bianca replied, using the witch's true name, denying her the identity she had chosen.

"That name did not work the last time. Neither will the magic you cast against me. This time you die."

As before, the air around Solomon shimmered and the smell of ozone filled the room.

Swinging her shotgun around, Bianca pointed at Solomon. The

witch smiled, as if amused that this small woman thought that her toy might hurt her.

Three times Bianca pulled the trigger. Three times shotshells delivered their deadly loads – flechettes mixed with the dirt from Solomon's grave. The small, sharp blades, powered by the soil in which Solomon had lain and a god's faith in her own weapon, cut the witch apart. The first shot removed most of a leg. The second and third shredded her chest.

Somehow Solomon survived. Somehow she still stood, gathering her strength, preparing to smite her enemy with the power of her god.

Bianca dropped her Mossberg. It had done its job. She drew Tromluí, slicing it at the witch's neck.

There was some resistance and Bianca felt the burning of Solomon's spell. But the power of the knife was too strong for the witch. Resistance faded and Solomon's head hit the floor even as Bianca stepped back to avoid the spray.

"You chose – poorly," the detective said to the corpse.

Bianca was near exhaustion, but there was still one more set of stairs to climb, at least one more enemy to face. Idly she wished for the war god's Elphane's spear, the one that always flies true. But she had lost her chance at wishing when she freed the genie and forgave his sins.

One step at a time, she climbed the stairs to meet her enemy.

The third floor was one big room. Dressed all in white, Apollonius sat in a high backed chair against the wall furthest from the stairs. Despite the darkness outside, the room was well lit although there were no obvious signs of illumination.

"I know you," said the seated figure. "You and that dark one interfered in Eire. And it may have been you that betrayed me to Caesar."

"That wasn't me," Bianca said, moving towards the Bright One with knife in hand. "I would not have involved the Romans. I do my own killing."

"Yet she was much like you, devoted to the tree god, the usurper, the false messiah."

Bianca edged closer. "That would be you."

"There is something of the one called Shaw about you," Apollonius said just before Bianca came into striking distance. "The knife you hold. It was his. It killed me. That time in Gotham. But not this time."

A wave of his hand. Bianca's hand, having begun to rise in a killing stroke, hung in the air. She tried to move but could not. Frozen in place, she could neither advance nor retreat.

This was not the Bright One's doing. Bianca knew this. Her fight, her acceptance of Bán had sensitized her to power and she had felt nothing come from the being in front of her.

DeWitt, you bastard, she thought as she realized the source of her paralysis.

Sorry, Sarge, but Apollonius ... he knew about my wife and kids. He threatened them.

What else? Bianca asked, sensing that Jackson was holding back.

He offered to ... give me back my life. To make me whole again. You have no idea what's it was like. I was always cold and alo...

Cut the crap, Judas. You were tempted and you fell and now you're just another piece of dirt.

Mentally cutting Jackson off, Bianca tried to think of a way out of her situation. There was the word Joe had given them, the one that would lay waste to the House. But would it work against a ghost and a god? If Apollonius ever let her speak she planned to find out.

"Betrayal is a terrible thing, is it not?" the Bright One asked. "The Nazarene was betrayed, as was I. And now you. It seems to be the lot of gods to have at least one false follower. But fear not, your death is far off. You dared to oppose me, small one. You killed my followers. You killed me. You cost me a kingdom. You will be a long time paying for that."

Apollonius followed this statement by explaining just how Bianca would pay – long term suffering; tortured physically, sexually, and mentally over a period of decades by both him and his many followers. She would cry out to her god but not be heard. She would beg for mercy but would receive none. She would curse the day her parents conceived her.

Bianca wasn't listening. Instead she focused on something Apollonius had said earlier. He had reminded her that she was a god. A god of vengeance, with a touch of Nightmare. And nightmares are dreams. And in dreams all things are possible.

And she was dreaming.

Bianca's body may have been paralyzed be her mind was free. And with her mind she sought for and found that part of Jackson that was inside her. She traced it back to the soul of the man she had once trusted.

Goodbye, Dewitt. Enjoy Hell.

Dewitt Jackson's spectral power was strong. But it was no match for the wrath of an angry god and a woman betrayed. With a thought Bianca ravaged his blackened soul the way her Mossberg had shredded the witch's body.

Then he was gone, banished from her body, evicted from the House, erased from existence. His final mental scream was one of regret, not for the sin of betrayal but of having made the wrong choice.

Her freeing herself and her banishing of Jackson had taken less time that it had seemed. The Bright One was still talking, speaking of the fresh hells he would create just for her and all those who opposed him.

Bianca lowered her arm.

He noticed her movement. Realizing that his hold over her had been broken he sought to use his power against her.

But in that house, in her dream, Bianca was a much a god as he was and it washed over her with no effect.

Just as any power she used would wash over him. As gods they were evenly matched.

But Bianca had a knife.

And a knife always works.

Slowly, calmly, Bianca walked up to Apollonius and placed Tromluí against his throat. He did not resist. He was beaten. He knew it and accepted his fate.

One push and it's all over, that part of Bianca that was Bán said.

Another part of her throught back to a house in northeast Baltimore, when with a squeeze of her trigger it would have been all over with Felix Manion. The same choice this time.

How well did that turn out? Bán asked.

Bianca ignored the voice. Manion had made his choice. So had Tavon. So would she. And so must Apollonius.

Removing the knife from the being's throat, Bianca stepped back, sheathed her weapon.

The Bright One was startled by this unexpected mercy. Before he could move,

"Get off that chair and I'll break your bones and kick your ass."

Believing her, he remained still as she spoke.

"We've beaten you three times now. As I understand it, that's the magic number. If so, you're finished in this world, in this time. If not, and you come back, you'll be beaten again. There will always be someone like the Nightmare or me to stop you. Because we're willing to sacrifice all to do it. What are you willing to sacrifice, other than those stupid or twisted enough to follow you? Are you willing to climb the Tree and accept the Nails? If not, then don't call yourself god or savior."

This was it. Bianca took a breath and prayed.

"Apollonius of Tyana, I offer you a choice – life or death. Choose the first, accept mortality and hope for salvation. Choose the second and face an uncertain eternity and probable damnation."

Sitting back in his chair, The Bright One pondered Bianca's offer. Finally,

"I can see why Morningstar fears you. The choices you offer… I have lived too long as what I am to become one of … them. You'll understand when you've been a god for a decade or two. Damnation though … I could not serve under the Devil's thumb. There would be war in Hell."

"One you couldn't win.'

"You think not?"

Bianca shook her head. "You lost three times against mortals. What chance do you think you'd have against demons and fallen angels?"

Apollonius shrugged. He made his choice. "Than that leaves only this."

Flying out of his chair, he lunged at Bianca, hoping to take her by surprise. But she had been a cop too long and knew never to trust a suspect not to do the stupid thing. Tromluí flew into her hand. As the Bright One crashed against her she shoved it just below his rib cage and tore downwards, leaving a wound not immediately fatal.

"Nice try, but you don't get to escape that easily. No more chances."

Holding Tromluí, leaving it in the dying god, Bianca used it as a connection between them, drawing his power into herself. When she was done, when all that was the Bright One was hers, she withdrew her blade and plunged it into his now mortal heart, sending him to whatever final judgment awaited him.

It's over, Bianca thought. Then it wasn't, as godly power raced through her being.

She saw them all, everyone who worshipped or followed the Bright One or had just though him cool. She knew Delilah Solomon's secret name. She knew what choices Felix Manion had made to make him who he was.

Her consciousness expanded beyond that. She could, if she wanted to, connect with anyone in the world – or everyone. She searched for Tammy and forgave her. She sought out Joe and reassured him. She looked into Genny Starr's heart and saw that despite the ordeals she had suffered she had not yet despaired but continued to hope in a higher power.

On that day Bianca Jones was the higher power. She found a way to help the girl.

We are a god, that part of her that was Bán told her. We can now mete out vengeance to all who deserve it.

We can torment their dreams and haunt their waking hours, said the nightmare inside her.

And I can make deserts bloom and food grow. I can end poverty and sickness and destroy the monsters among us, and Joe and I can find peace.

But no sooner had Bianca finished this thought then she knew it was not to be. There would be one monster left, the one who claimed a godhood, the one who, in a decade or two, might come to see those she sought to rule as "them."

When you fight monsters, you risk becoming one. And when you fight gods …

With her expanded consciousness, Bianca gazed into the Source from which her powers came. And the Source gazed back into her. She saw her Tree and felt her Nails and knew that she was not worthy to accept them.

Humbled, Bianca said farewell to Bán then willingly released the power inside her, returning it to the Source, saving only enough to lift whatever curse afflicted the House.

Her power faded. The House became just a house and Tromluí just another knife.

Bianca woke. Tromluí was in its sheath and her bags and weapons beside her bed. Her radio alarm was blaring the news of how a sick imposter had posed as Ginny Starr and posted faked videos and images of America's Girlfriend over all of cyberspace.

She smiled. Beat you again, you bastard. Then she called Joe.

"It's over," she said when her love answered his phone. "Come home to me."

Biography

JOHN L. FRENCH has worked for over thirty-five years as a crime scene investigator and has seen more than his share of murders, shootings, and serious assaults. As a break from the realities of his job, he writes science fiction, pulp, horror, fantasy, and, of course, crime fiction.

In 1992 John began writing stories based on his training and experiences on the streets of Baltimore. His first story "Past Sins" was published in Hardboiled Magazine and was cited as one of the best Hardboiled stories of 1993. More crime fiction followed, appearing in Alfred Hitchcock's Mystery Magazine, the Fading Shadows magazines and in collections by Barnes and Noble. Association with writers like James Chambers and the late, great C.J. Henderson led him to try horror fiction and to a still growing fascination with zombies and other undead things. His first horror story "The Right Solution" appeared in Marietta Publishing's Lin Carter's Anton Zarnak. Other horror stories followed in anthologies such as The Dead Walk and Dark Furies, both published by Die Monster Die books. It was in Dark Furies that Bianca Jones made her literary debut in "21 Doors," a story based on an old Baltimore legend and a creepy game his daughter used to play with her friends.

John's first book was The Devil of Harbor City, a novel done in the old pulp style. Past Sins and Here There Be Monsters soon followed. John was also consulting editor for Chelsea House's Criminal Investigation series. His other books include The Assassins' Ball (Written with Patrick Thomas), Paradise Denied, Blood Is the Life and The Nightmare Strikes. John is the editor of To Hell In A Fast Car, Mermaids 13, C. J. Henderson's Challenge of the Unknown, and (with Greg Schauer) With Great Power...

TALES FROM THE SEA
MERMAIDS
13
Edited by
John L. French

APOCALYPSE
13
THIRTEEN FANTASTICAL
TALES FOR THE END OF DAYS
ANTHOLOGY
DEFCON 1
...WARNING...
MISSILE LAUNCH
EDITED BY
DIANE RAETZ

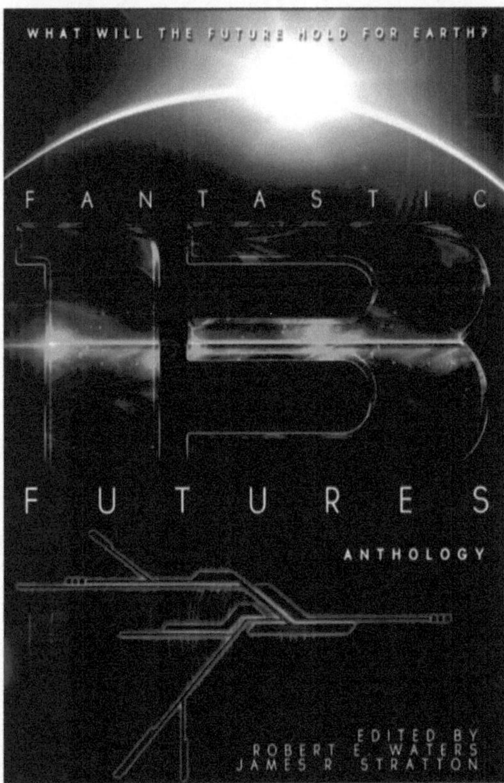

WHAT WILL THE FUTURE HOLD FOR EARTH?
FANTASTIC
13
FUTURES
ANTHOLOGY
EDITED BY
ROBERT E. WATERS
JAMES R STRATTON

EDITED BY EDWARD J. MCFADDEN III
LUCKY
13
Thirteen Tales of
Crime & Mayhem
Good or bad, it runs out eventually.
It's all just a matter of luck.
FEATURING
Trent Zelazny
Jessica McHugh
Matt Schairiti
Sarah A. Hoyt
Brady Allen
Danielle Ackley-McPhail
Patrick Thomas
Robert E. Waters
G. Elmer Munson
Diane Raetz
Georgina Morales
John L. French
Michael Laimo